"Is it an office job you've got in mind?" Deborah asked

"Partly." Gil sounded annoyed at having his train of thought interrupted. "It would involve some entertaining, too."

"I wouldn't mind doing that." Anything would be better than arriving in Parang late that night without a single rupiah in her pocket! "What exactly is the job?"

Gil put down the fork he had been fiddling with and looked at her with his direct, disconcertingly pale stare.

"I need a wife," he said.

Jessica Hart was born in Ghana, but grew up in an Oxfordshire village. Her father was a civil engineer working overseas, so by the time she left school, she'd been to East Africa, South Africa, Papua New Guinea and Oman—and had acquired incurably itchy feet. She's had a haphazard series of jobs, including production assistant at a theater, research assistant, waitress, English teacher, cook on an outback property—in England, Egypt, Kenya, Jakarta and Australia, respectively. Jessica now lives in England, where her hobbies are limited to eating, drinking and traveling, preferably to places where she'll find good food or desert or tropical rain.

Don't miss any of our special offers. Write to us at the following address for information on our newest releases.

Harlequin Reader Service
U.S.: 3010 Walden Ave., P.O. Box 1325, Buffalo, NY 14269
Canadian: P.O. Box 609, Fort Erie, Ont. L2A 5X3

A SENSIBLE WIFE
Jessica Hart

Harlequin Books

TORONTO • NEW YORK • LONDON
AMSTERDAM • PARIS • SYDNEY • HAMBURG
STOCKHOLM • ATHENS • TOKYO • MILAN
MADRID • WARSAW • BUDAPEST • AUCKLAND

ISBN 0-373-03334-6

A SENSIBLE WIFE

This edition published by arrangement with Harlequin Enterprises B. V.

® and TM are trademarks of the publisher. Trademarks indicated with ® are registered in the United States Patent and Trademark Office, the Canadian Trade Marks Office and in other countries.

Printed in U.S.A.

CHAPTER ONE

DEBORAH pulled down the window as far as it would go and leant out. Perhaps if she concentrated on the view it would take her mind off the thought of lunch.

She had been sleeping so heavily that she hadn't even realised that the jolting, lurching bus had stopped until the driver had shaken her awake and gestured at the ramshackle restaurant at the roadside to indicate a lunch stop. She wished that he hadn't woken her. She had so little money left that she had decided to skip lunch, but now her stomach rumbled in protest as the appetisingly spicy smells of Indonesian cooking wafted over from the tables where her fellow passengers were cheerfully tucking into plates of *nasi goreng*.

Resolutely averting her eyes, Deborah sighed. She was addicted to the Indonesian version of fried rice, made with hot chillies and onions and numerous other ingredients which she preferred not to identify, and her mouth watered at the idea of throwing caution to the wind and ordering a plateful for herself.

'I must be sensible,' she told herself firmly. She had barely enough money to get the ferry back to Java without wasting it on a lunch she didn't *really* need. Here she was, high in the hills of Serok, one of the wilder and more remote of Indonesia's thirteen thousand islands; surely she shouldn't be wasting her time thinking about lunch?

It was certainly a magnificent view. The restaurant, a rudimentary collection of tables and benches under an awning, was perched on the edge of a hillside, overlooking an awe-inspiring valley. Far below, the river was a faint gleam of silver in the sun, overwhelmed by the jungle-clad mountains looming on either side.

Resting her folded arms on the window, Deborah wondered why on earth someone had chosen to set up a restaurant just here. It wasn't as if they could get a lot of custom. The empty road wound round the contour of the hill and disappeared once more into the rain forest, leaving the little restaurant the only sign of civilisation in the vast expanse of damp, dark, tangled green.

There was only one other vehicle parked next to the bus. It was a rather smart four-wheel-drive, and Deborah eyed it nearly as enviously as she had the plates of *nasi goreng*. Travelling on local buses was cheap and fun, but, after several hours of sleeping uncomfortably jammed between the window and a woman trying to balance two children and a basket of squawking chickens on her lap, a private car represented the height of luxury.

It would be air-conditioned, too, Deborah thought, a touch wistfully. Even this high in the hills, the air was hot and oppressively humid, and she lifted her heavy plait in a vain effort to cool her neck. She glanced over at the tables to see if she could identify the lucky owner.

It wasn't hard to guess. A European man was standing by a table paying his bill. He looked utterly detached from the cheerful hubbub going on around him, and as Deborah blew a stray strand of dark hair away from her face she wondered how he managed to look so neat and cool in the stifling humidity.

As she watched, he nodded farewell to the waiter and walked towards the car. He had a quick, purposeful tread that set him apart from the more languidly graceful Indonesians even more than the colour of his skin.

Deborah's stomach groaned alarmingly, reminding her yet again that she hadn't eaten since lunch the day before, and she fixed her gaze on the man in an attempt to divert her mind from veering back to food. He had to be English, she bet herself. He had dark brown hair and an angular, rather watchful face, and there was a coolly competent, understated air about him that was somehow quintessentially English.

He glanced indifferently at the bus as he passed, and if he noticed the dishevelled girl hanging out of the window he gave no sign of it. Deborah, a little disappointed at being so comprehensively ignored, got the impression of a man with a major problem on his mind. His dark brows were drawn together, and his expression was preoccupied as he opened the back of the car and pulled a briefcase towards him.

Deborah studied him, impressed despite herself by the controlled economy of his movements. There was a steadiness about him, a sense of self-sufficiency that gave him an unmistakable presence. She guessed that he was in his mid-thirties, but he had the quiet authority of an older man.

What was he doing here? The crisp short-sleeved white shirt and dark trousers certainly weren't holiday gear, and anyway he was too businesslike to be on holiday. He might be a doctor, she decided. He had the right kind of reassuringly capable air, but, peering inside the car, she couldn't see any sign of a medical bag. She ruled out businessman as well: he looked too tough. She couldn't imagine him sitting behind a desk all day. He didn't look the diplomatic type either, unless he was on some secret mission. Yes, he might be a spy, thought Deborah, amused by her fanciful speculations. It was a favourite game of hers; she had whiled away many idle hours at bus stations and border crossings inventing backgrounds for people. That steely quality, the sense of controlled strength, the subtle air of command, even the rather alarming reserve . . . they all fitted.

She was deciding what his mission was when he looked at his watch and banged the boot shut. He had some papers under his arm as he came back to the front of the car. Carried away by her imagination, Deborah's blue eyes followed him speculatively, and she was unprepared for him to stop suddenly and look up at her.

She found herself staring into eyes that were cool and grey and startlingly light against his tan, and her heart gave an odd lurch, as if she had jumped suddenly into icy water.

'Is something wrong?' he asked, his voice as cold as his eyes.

'No,' said Deborah, surprised, but gratified to discover that he was as uncompromisingly English as she had guessed.

'Then may I ask why you've been staring at me—
or is there something particularly fascinating about
opening the back of a car?'

Another girl might have denied that she had been
watching him, but it never occurred to Deborah.
'You see, I'm trying not to think about lunch,' she
confided.

'I hardly think that staring at me is going to help,'
he said nastily. 'Why don't you look at the view
instead?'

'I would, but it's not nearly so distracting when
you're hungry,' Deborah explained. 'People are
always much more interesting than scenery,
anyway.'

'At least you know where you are with the land-
scape. You don't have to wonder if it's really all it
seems, the way you do with people.'

'But that's exactly what's so interesting about
people,' said Deborah, wondering what memory
had brought that bitter edge to his voice. 'I forgot
all about lunch while I was wondering about you.
I guessed you were English straight away,' she added
triumphantly, 'and I was just deciding what you
were doing here.'

'And what conclusion did you come to?' he asked
in a dry voice.

Deborah's untidy plait hung over her shoulder
as she leant forward confidentially, and her blue
eyes danced with teasing humour. 'I thought you
might be . . . you know, on a special mission.' She
tapped the side of her nose in a knowing gesture.

He wasn't amused. 'I hate to disappoint you,' he
said with some sarcasm, 'but I'm afraid I'm just a
civil engineer.'

'Oh.' Deborah digested the information. He looked like a man who liked everything arranged in straight, orderly lines. 'I should have guessed,' she said frankly.

The man opened the driver's door. 'Now you know, perhaps you'd stop staring at me? I want to finish reading this report before I go on, and I'm not in the mood for any distractions.'

Without waiting for her reply, he got in, shut the door and switched on the engine to start the air-conditioning.

Deborah withdrew her head and slumped back into her seat. She felt oddly deflated, as if she had been dismissed. Glancing out of the window, she saw that he was absorbed in his report. He had evidently put her out of his mind without any difficulty. It was all right for him to say he didn't need any distractions, Deborah thought crossly. He'd had *his* lunch.

She folded her arms and glowered at the back of the battered seat in front of her. He might have been a bit more friendly. It wasn't as if she had been doing any harm, and now she would have to find something else to take her mind off food.

The rain forest lay stretched out below her, humming with life, but from where she sat it was impossible to see anything beneath the impenetrable tree canopy. She watched a large hornbill glide silently across the valley and disappear into the branches, but her attention was still on the man sitting in the car next to her. Having noticed him, he was the kind of man you somehow went on noticing. It was very annoying.

Oh, to hell with it! There was no point in sitting here wondering about him. She would go and have something to eat and worry about how to pay for somewhere to stay when she got to Parang. Jumping to her feet, Deborah reached up to the overhead rack for her bag.

It wasn't there. It wasn't on the rack, nor was it under the seats when she checked frantically. A cold hand closed about her heart. She had definitely put it on the rack, and it had been firmly wedged there. It couldn't possibly have fallen off, but she looked along the bus just in case. It had gone.

'Don't panic!' she said out loud, clutching her head. Just because the bag had contained all her money, her passport and her onward ticket to Australia, there was absolutely no reason to panic.

Deborah panicked. With the vague thought of finding the driver in case someone had handed in her bag, she ran down the bus and went hurtling down the steps at the side just as the Englishman's car pulled away from its parking place.

She cannoned into the bonnet, knocking her knee and winding herself badly, but she was saved from worse injury by his lightning reactions. He had stamped on the brakes, and their protesting squeal seemed to echo in the air as Deborah collapsed over the bonnet trying to get her breath.

'Of all the stupid things to do!' He was out of the car in a flash and jerking her upright with a hard hand. 'Are you all right?'

'I—I think so.' Deborah was shaken by the cold fury in his eyes as much as by the near-accident.

'You don't deserve to be!' He dropped his hand in disgust, and without his support she sank weakly back against the car, her legs too shaky to support her. 'Have you got some kind of death wish, or did you think you'd throw yourself under a car to take your mind off lunch too?'

'I didn't see you,' Deborah said, rubbing her knee.

'You mean you didn't look!' he snapped. 'Why on earth couldn't you climb down off the bus like any normal person instead of flinging yourself off?'

Deborah's panic, momentarily knocked out of her with her breath when she collided with the car, came back with a rush. 'I've lost my bag,' she said wildly, and forced herself to stand upright as she spotted the driver in the distance. She had to get to him and find out if he had seen what had happened to her bag, but the Englishman was blocking her way, still glaring at her in exasperation.

'You nearly lost a lot more than your bag!' He looked down into dismayed blue eyes. 'Are you sure you've lost it?' he asked brusquely, as if irritated at having succumbed to her helplessness.

'Well, yes . . . I mean, I can't see it, and I *know* I put it up there——'

He took her arm in an iron grip. 'Calm down!' he ordered, and the hard voice had far more effect than warm sympathy would have done. Deborah took a deep breath. 'That's better,' he said. 'Rushing around like a maniac won't solve anything. Where were you going in such a hurry, anyway?'

'I thought the driver might have seen something. Or someone might have handed it to him when they realised they'd picked up the wrong bag.'

'I think that's highly unlikely,' he said with a sardonic expression.

'I can't think of anything else to do!'

He sighed irritably. 'I suppose I'd better have a look in case you've missed it. Show me where you were sitting.'

Deborah was inclined to resent his abrupt attitude, but she found herself doing exactly as he had ordered. 'It was up there, on the rack.' She pointed the place out to him when she had described the bag.

He grunted. 'You should have noticed if anyone had lifted it down, then.'

'Yes, but I was asleep most of the time,' she explained. 'And I couldn't see much because of the chickens.'

'Chickens?' He looked at her as if she'd gone mad.

'The woman next to me had a huge basket on her lap,' she explained, and picked a feather off the seat as if to demonstrate that she was telling the truth.

'I see,' the man said drily. 'Well, I can't see anything like your bag. We can have a word with the driver, but I think you'd better resign yourself to its loss. I presume it didn't have anything valuable in it?'

'My purse,' said Deborah, her blood running cold as the full impact of what she had lost hit her. 'And my passport...and my plane ticket...oh, God, and my camera!' she wailed, wringing her hands. Her eyes were huge in her distraught face as she looked at him in despair. 'What am I going to do?'

He was staring at her incredulously. 'Let me get this right. You put all your valuables in one bag, threw it on to a rack on a crowded bus where anyone could help themselves to it and then went to sleep?'

'Er—yes.' She felt very small and very stupid when he put it like that.

'Why didn't you just throw them out of the window?' he demanded with a snort of exasperated disbelief. 'That would have been just as good a way of getting rid of them! Didn't it occur to you that it might be a good idea to keep your money and passport on your lap?'

'I did at first,' said Deborah, on the defensive. 'But then that lady sat down next to me, and she had so much to carry that I thought the least I could do was offer to have one of the children on my lap, and then we squeezed up so that the other one could sit between us, and what with the chickens there simply wasn't room for my bag, so I had to put it on the rack.'

He gave an exasperated sigh. 'I'm sure it was much more comfortable for you all, but you seem to have been left with a bit of a problem, don't you?'

Deborah's hands twisted together as she battled to suppress her rising panic. 'What am I going to do?' she whimpered again. 'No passport, no money, no ticket . . . I'm completely stuck!' Wild thoughts of falling into the clutches of the white slave trade spun through her mind. 'I'll never get to Australia now . . . will I ever even get home? I might never see my family again!' she moaned despairingly, as her imagination presented her with increasingly hideous visions of her future, and a twinge of hunger seemed to set the seal on her doom. 'I'm never going to get any lunch now,' she realised irrelevantly.

'I would have thought lunch would be the least of your problems,' the man said caustically, and when Deborah began gnawing at her fingernails he gave an impatient sigh. 'Look, there's no point in panicking. You've just got to face the situation and do something about it,' he said sternly, and Deborah thought bitterly that it was easy enough for him to say. He wasn't facing the prospect of being stranded in the middle of nowhere!

Still, when he climbed down the steps of the bus, she found herself following him as if he was her one security. 'I don't see what I can do,' she said, beginning to flap again.

'You could have a word with the driver, for a start. It's unlikely, but he might know something.' He frowned at her. 'Do you speak Indonesian?'

'I can say good morning and thank you, things like that,' she said, feeling more inadequate than ever.

'That's not going to get you very far, is it?' He looked disapprovingly at the warm, chaotic girl who stood beside him, her dishevelled hair escaping wildly from her plait and her clothes crumpled and travel-stained. 'What on earth are you doing travelling in a place like this on your own? They shouldn't let girls like you out of the country unless you've got a certificate of competence, and I very much doubt if you would qualify!'

'I've been coping perfectly well!' said Deborah, stung into indignant defence.

'If you can call being stranded in the middle of nowhere without money, passport or onward ticket "coping perfectly well"!' he retorted sarcastically. He ran his fingers through his hair irritably as he watched her face flush with mortification. 'I suppose I could talk to the driver for you,' he offered brusquely.

'Would you?' In spite of his impatient manner, Deborah's face lit with a radiant smile of relief. 'Thank you so much!'

Deborah wasn't a strictly pretty girl, but she had so much personality that few people noticed that her nose was slightly crooked and her mouth too wide. Her cornflower-blue eyes sparkled with warmth and humour and when she smiled she had an arresting quality that went beyond mere prettiness to unexpected beauty.

The Englishman raised an eyebrow as if taken aback by the abrupt transformation, but he only said gruffly, 'You wait here.'

Too nervous to sit still, Deborah paced up and down as she watched him stride over to the driver. He wasn't the most charming of knights on white chargers, but there was something very reassuring about his brisk competence, and she found that she was clinging to the thought of him as her only defence against overwhelming panic. When he came back, she had to stop herself running towards him as if he was her last hope.

'Well?' she asked eagerly.

He shook his head. 'The driver doesn't know anything,' he said, putting his hands in his pockets. 'Not that I expected he would! Unfortunately, it doesn't make your position any easier.' He frowned down at her as if she was a particularly irritating problem, as Deborah supposed she was. 'What are you going to do now?'

'I don't know,' said Deborah honestly. Biting her thumb, she tried to think calmly. 'I expect he'll take me as far as Parang, won't he? After all, he saw my ticket when I got on, so he knows I've paid my fare.'

'And what then?'

'Well . . . I might be able to find a job teaching English,' she suggested without much optimism, while her stomach churned at the thought of what her alternatives might be.

The Englishman was dismissive of her attempt to appear as if she had thought sensibly about her situation. 'In *Parang*?' he echoed. 'I hope you're joking! Any girl would be easy prey in a rough town like Parang, let alone one without money or apparent common sense.'

Deborah clasped her hands together to stop them shaking. 'What else can I do?' she asked in a wobbly voice, horribly afraid that she was going to burst into tears. She saw him glance impatiently at his watch and tried to pull herself together. 'You're in a hurry . . . I'm sorry if I held you up,' she wavered and took a deep breath. 'I'm sure I'll find something,' she said in a steadier voice. 'You don't have to worry about me.'

'I can hardly drive off and leave you planning to go wandering down to a place like Parang on your own,' he said angrily.

Deborah opened her mouth to reply, but her stomach got in first with an embarrassingly loud rumble. She blushed, and clapped her hand guiltily over her stomach as if to silence it.

He sighed. 'For heaven's sake, come and have something to eat! You're obviously not going to concentrate on your problems until you've had your lunch!'

'You mustn't stay for me. I'm not your problem.' Deborah hung back, in spite of the tantalising prospect of food. 'I'll be fine.'

'I wish I could believe that!' Evidently deciding he wasn't going to waste any more time persuading her, he seized her wrist and marched her over to a table, where he pushed her on to a bench without ceremony and called a brisk order over to the waiter.

'It's very kind of you,' said Deborah in a small voice, rubbing her wrist. He didn't look that big but he had a grip like steel.

'I don't feel very kind,' he said, sitting down opposite her and regarding her dishevelled state with some disapproval. 'The sooner I get you sorted out, the sooner I can be on my way with a clear conscience.'

There was a rather awkward pause. 'Where are you going?' Deborah said at last, feeling that the least she could do was make an effort at polite conversation—not that this man seemed overly concerned with politeness!

'The Terawati valley,' he said briefly, and reached into the pocket of his shirt and handed her a business card. 'I suppose we'd better introduce ourselves.'

'Gil Hamilton, Hamilton Douviers, Tanah Terawati Hydro-Electric Project,' she read. 'I'm

Deborah,' she added, handing him back the card. 'Deborah Clarke.'

She was unprepared for his reaction. The card dropped from his hand and he stared at her in amazement. '*What* did you say your name was?'

'Deborah Clarke,' she repeated, baffled. 'Is something the matter?'

'No.' Clearly making an effort to pull himself together, Gil Hamilton picked the card up from the table and replaced it in his pocket with a frown. 'Just an extraordinary coincidence, that's all.'

Deborah stared at him. It wasn't as if it was an unusual name—quite the opposite. She had always wanted to be called something exotic like Jade or Storm, instead of plain old Deborah. She waited for Gil Hamilton to explain the coincidence, but he seemed to have forgotten she was there. He was frowning at the saucer of chillies that sat on every restaurant table, as if he was turning something important over in his mind.

Not daring to interrupt him, Deborah leant her folded arms on the table and contemplated the spectacular view of the jungle valley. Wraiths of mist still clung to the canopy, stubbornly resisting the midday sun, and somewhere below them an unseen bird called raucously to its mate across the forest.

'It's beautiful here, isn't it?' she sighed, forgetting her predicament for a moment. She was a tall, slender girl, with thick dark brown hair tied back from her face in a plait that looked much the worse for wear after the long bus journey. Her blue eyes were dreamy and the generous mouth curved into a contented smile that faltered as she glanced back at Gil Hamilton to find him watching her with a peculiarly speculative expression.

'I thought you didn't like looking at views,' he said.

'I didn't say that I didn't like them,' said Deborah, beaming up at the waiter who was placing an enormous plate of fried rice in front of her. She picked up a spoon and fork with a sigh of anticipation. 'I just said they weren't distracting enough when you're trying to take your mind off something.'

'Well, I hope you're not letting the view distract you from the problem in hand,' he said severely.

'No.' Deborah's smile vanished. 'I've got to find some way of earning myself enough money to get to the British Embassy in Jakarta so that I can get a new passport, I suppose.'

'You can put Parang out of your mind, if you're still thinking about going there,' he said flatly.

'Well, I can't go back to Jatipakan. I've just come from there.'

'What on earth were you doing *there*?'

'I'd always wanted to come to Serok,' she explained, her face lighting up as she laid down her spoon and fork. 'It's so wild and steamy and exotic, and nobody seems to know anything about it. I met someone in Yogyakarta who told me there were some English teaching jobs going in Jatipakan, so I used practically all the money I had left getting up there.' She picked up her cutlery again and carried on with her *nasi goreng*. 'I suppose I should have been suspicious of how quick they were to offer me a job. When I started work I found out I had to teach huge classes crammed into a tiny room, and the only materials I had were a crummy black-board and a piece of chalk. There was no way they were going to learn any English! Then I found out that the pay was all tied up with what were called ''extra tasks'', and it didn't take much to work out what they were for the female teachers! I'd signed a contract, but I didn't think they could do much about it if I'd gone, so I got on the first bus to Parang and, well, here I am.'

Gil Hamilton was profoundly unimpressed by her story. 'You're not fit to be wandering around on your own in a place like this. You're lucky you didn't get into real trouble—not that you aren't in enough trouble as it is!'

Deborah concentrated on her rice. She didn't feel in a strong enough position to argue, and after a moment he asked abruptly, 'Is your name really Deborah Clarke?'

'Of course it is!' she said indignantly. 'Why would I lie about something like that?'

'Women will lie about anything,' he said in a harsh voice.

'Well, *I* don't!'

'That's rather a shame, as I was beginning to wonder if our meeting might not have been rather providential. I was going to offer you a job, but it would need someone who was prepared to take part in a pretence where a strict regard for the truth might be a little inhibiting.' He paused. His light, clear eyes rested on her face and an odd feeling shivered down Deborah's spine. 'I thought that anyone who was capable of inventing a story about me being a spy might be able to enter a little play-acting without too much difficulty.'

'I don't mind *pretending*,' Deborah said quickly, anxious not to lose the chance of a job. 'I'll do it.'

Gil frowned. 'Don't you think it would be a good idea to find out what the job is before you commit yourself to anything?'

'I'll do anything,' she said simply. 'I don't mind.'

He looked irritated by her reckless attitude. 'Can you type?'

'Yes,' she said, mentally crossing her fingers. 'I used to work as a temp in London.' No point in telling him what a terrible secretary she had been! Her spelling was atrocious and her typing wildly inaccurate, but she had almost always been asked to stay on as she got on so well with everyone.

'So you do know something about office work?'

'Oh, yes.' She gave him a breezy smile.

'Hmmm.' Gil sounded unconvinced. He was frowning as he stared down at the fork he was turning between square, capable-looking hands. The piercingly light eyes were shielded, leaving Deborah free to study him properly. He had an austere, intelligent face with a stubborn set to the jaw. His expression was grim, and she wondered what it was that had put him in such a bad mood. He didn't look as if he was always this forbidding. There were laughter-lines around his eyes and an intriguing curl to the corners of his mouth. It was a nice mouth, she decided, cool and uncompromising like the rest of him but with an unexpected hint of sensuousness. Just looking at it gave her a strange feeling in the pit of her stomach, and she looked away quickly.

'How long have you been travelling?' he asked abruptly.

'About seven months.' Deborah toyed with her fork and tried to stop thinking about Gil's mouth. 'It took me over a year to save enough money to come away. I worked as a temp during the day and in the evenings I was a waitress in a wine bar, but it was worth it to be able to travel.' She sighed. 'I was on my way to Australia, but I don't suppose I'll ever get there now that I've lost my onward ticket.'

Gil grunted. 'It sounds as if you're not afraid of hard work, anyway,' he commented with grudging approval. 'Do you always travel on your own?' he asked, and Deborah had the feeling he was testing her in some way. She nodded.

'You meet more people on your own,' she explained. 'Sometimes friends say they'd like to come with me, but they can't really be bothered to save the money, or they're too involved with their careers to take time off work, or they don't want to go anywhere where they can't get a hot shower...' She shrugged. 'It's better to be independent.'

'So there's no boyfriend waiting patiently for you to come home?'

'No.' Deborah looked at him curiously, wondering where all this was leading. 'I never seem to get very involved with anyone, because I'm always planning my next trip.'

'Travelling alone can be a risky business, as you've just found out,' Gil said with a touch of disapproval. 'Don't you ever worry about what might happen?'

Deborah sighed. 'There seem to be so many people at home worrying about me that there never seems any point in me worrying too. Every time I go away, they're all convinced they're never going to see me again! I know it means they care for me, but sometimes all the worrying seems excessive. My friends worry, my family worry...the dog probably worries too.'

'With good reason, from what I've seen of you so far,' Gil said astringently, and Deborah bit her lip.

'Nothing like this has ever happened to me before,' she said, but his comment had reminded her once more of her precarious situation. She was doing plenty of worrying of her own now!

Gil had lapsed into silence once more, and she eyed him anxiously. If he really *could* offer her a job, it would solve all her problems.

'Is it an office job you've got in mind?' she asked at last, unable to bear the suspense any longer.

'Partly.' He sounded annoyed at having his train of thought interrupted. 'It would involve some entertaining too.'

'It sounds fun.' Unable to scrape any more rice off the plate, Deborah pushed it reluctantly aside and took a sip of the grainy Indonesian coffee that always seemed to come served in a tall glass. 'I wouldn't mind doing that.' Anything would be better than arriving in Parang late tonight without a single rupiah in her pocket! 'What exactly is the job?'

Gil put down the fork he had been fiddling with and looked at her with his direct, disconcertingly pale stare.

'I need a wife,' he said.

CHAPTER TWO

DEBORAH choked, spraying coffee inelegantly over the table. 'What?' she coughed. 'You're not serious?'

'I'm not in a joking mood,' he snapped. 'You want a job, don't you?'

'Getting married qualifies as a bit more than a job!'

'I don't want to marry you.' Gil cast a disparaging look at her grubby red shirt and faded jeans. 'Heaven forbid!'

Deborah, still reeling from the shock of his announcement, was surprised at how hurt she was by his evident disgust. 'You said you needed a wife.'

'I need someone to pretend to be my wife,' he corrected her. 'It's not exactly the same thing.'

'But...' Deborah opened her mouth, then closed it. 'Why?' she asked eventually.

Gil took a little time replying, as if he was trying to sort his thoughts. 'I'm an engineer, as you know,' he began. 'I've recently established my own firm in partnership with a Frenchman called Pascal Douviers. The idea is to harness the best of the British and French expertise in one team, and although we've had a number of successful designs in Europe the Tanah Terawati scheme is our first major project. It's our chance to break into the big league, and a lot depends on whether the Indonesian government awards us the contract to build the next stage of the scheme. That means that Pascal and I are both working at Terawati at the moment. There's a lot of work to do preparing our proposal, but if we secure the contract Pascal will stay in Indonesia while I move on to troubleshoot round other projects.'

'Yes, but what's this got to do with your needing a wife?' Deborah burst out, unable to contain herself any longer. She had expected Gil to need a secretary, an administrator, a cook, perhaps . . . but a *wife*?

'I'm just coming to that,' he said irritably. 'You need to know the background. This is a very important time for the firm.'

Deborah was alarmed at how vividly she could imagine being this stranger's wife. She didn't know anything about him, other than the fact that he was brusque and competent. How could she even consider such a proposal? He might be a vicious monster, for all she knew, but when she looked at the cool, clean lines of his face it was hard to believe. He looked like a man who knew the meaning of old-fashioned words like 'integrity' and 'honour'. 'So what's the problem?' she said, trying to sound brisk.

'The problem is Pascal's wife, Sylvie.' He hesitated so long that Deborah had to prompt him.

'Well?'

'Sylvie is a very attractive woman,' he said carefully. 'Unfortunately, she's also very bored. I told Pascal it would be a mistake to bring a woman to a remote site like Terawati, but he didn't want to leave her alone in France any longer.'

'That's understandable, surely?'

'An engineer's wife has got to learn to accept separations.' Gil was unsympathetic. 'They ought to realise before they get married that their husbands will often be working in places that are quite unsuitable for women. My fiancée and I have put off our own wedding for precisely that reason.'

Deborah had been twirling the glass between her hands while she listened, but now she put it down on the plastic tablecloth with a sharp click. 'Your fiancée?' she repeated, unwilling to analyse a strangely sinking sensation. 'If you've got a fiancée already, why do you need another wife?'

'If you'd stop interrupting, I might be able to explain!' Gil rubbed his hand over his jaw. 'As I was trying to tell you, Pascal and I worked well together until Sylvie came out. Pascal spent most of his time up on the dam site, and I liaised with the government, doing most of the paperwork in the office. We've been trying to keep our expenses down, so I didn't bring a secretary out from our head office in London. I thought we could make do with local staff, but recently the pressure's been on to get the proposal for stage two ready in time, and Sylvie's been insisting on helping out.'

Deborah's head was in a whirl. She tried to concentrate on what he was saying but she wanted to scream, Fiancée? What fiancée? What was she like?

With an effort, Deborah brought her mind back to Gil's problem. 'What's wrong with that?'

'Nothing,' said Gil, 'except that she's being a little too helpful. Pascal's often away on site for a few days at a time, and Sylvie always seemed to be around, hanging around the office, dropping into my house at night, asking me round for dinner...'

He looked away down the valley. 'It was all getting a little embarrassing.'

'Oh, I *see*,' said Deborah. 'You mean she's got the hots for you?'

'I wouldn't have put it in quite such a vulgar way, but yes, that's about it. Naturally, it put me in a very awkward position. I couldn't be openly rude to her. I couldn't even suggest that I knew what she was doing, as she would no doubt have denied everything. She's Pascal's wife, and I can't allow anything to prejudice our partnership at this crucial time.'

'I can see that it must have been rather difficult,' said Deborah, wondering how Sylvie had ever had the nerve to try and seduce this formidable man. She must be very confident of her own charms. 'What did you do?'

'I talked about my fiancée a lot, much more than I would have done otherwise. She's a secretary—a very efficient one—and eventually it occurred to me that the best thing I could do was marry her now and bring her out with me when I came back from a design conference in London this time. I've only got another three months here, whether we win the contract or not, so she wouldn't have to spend too long here, and of course she could use her secretarial skills, which would keep Sylvie out of the office. It was ideal, really, as we wouldn't have to make all the special arrangements for accommodation that bringing a single secretary out from London would have entailed. I thought that having a wife on site would be the most effective way of keeping everything civilised for the last few months, and there would be no chance of any embarrassing scenes that Pascal might get to hear about.'

'It seems rather a cold-blooded reason to get married,' Deborah commented with her usual frankness. 'I thought people were supposed to get married because they couldn't bear to live without each other, not to provide secretarial services and keep nymphomaniac wives away!'

'We're both practical people,' Gil said with a cold look. 'Fortunately Debbie doesn't share your tendency to over-romanticise.'

'Debbie?' said Deborah, in a hollow voice. 'Is that your fiancée's name?'

He nodded. 'She's a Debra too, but she's always called Debbie.'

'Quite a coincidence,' she said, feeling that some comment was called for.

'It's more of a coincidence than you think,' said Gil. 'I don't know about the spelling, but her name's exactly the same as yours: Debra Clark. No doubt you can see where you come in now.'

'I must be very stupid, but no, I can't.' A quite unreasonable jealousy of the unknown Debbie, whom Gil talked about in such an intimate way, sharpened Deborah's voice. 'Why can't Debbie come out and keep Sylvie out of your hair if she's so practical?'

His eyes didn't quite meet hers. 'I wrote to Debbie, of course, before I left for London. We'd talked about getting married on several occasions, but it had always seemed more sensible to put it off. I rather assumed that she would see the practicalities of getting married now.'

'Obviously she didn't see it that way,' said Deborah, who was not exactly surprised. It didn't matter how sensible a girl was, she still wouldn't like her wedding reduced to a matter of practicalities. Still, if she had really loved him, surely she would have married him regardless? Gil Hamilton wasn't the kind of man you would want to let go.

'She said she wanted more time to plan the wedding,' said Gil, not quite managing to hide the bitterness in his voice. 'And she wasn't very impressed when I showed her some photos of Terawati and the bungalow. She said she'd rather stick to our original plan of buying a house in London that I would use as a base between travelling.'

It didn't sound like much of a relationship to Deborah, and she glanced at Gil, wondering just how hurt he had been by Debbie's refusal to fall in with his plans. He didn't give much away, with his cool, quiet face and his cool, quiet mouth, but presumably there were deeper feelings beneath that grimly self-possessed exterior.

'So she wouldn't come?'

'No.' Gil looked back at her at last. 'They'll be expecting me to turn up at the camp tonight with a new bride. I could say that she wasn't well enough to come out, but of course that won't solve the problem of Sylvie.'

'Or?' said Deborah, her heart beginning to beat a little faster.

'Or you could come with me,' he said, leaning forward persuasively. 'Nobody would know that you weren't the right Debra Clark. I could introduce you as my wife, and your presence for the last three months would make things a lot easier all round. I also badly need a secretary and I'd rather not have to rely on Sylvie, with all the complications that would involve. It would be a strictly business arrangement, of course. I'd pay you a good salary for all this, and at the end of three months you'd have enough to get yourself to Jakarta and even to carry on with whatever you were doing.'

Deborah's stomach was alive with butterflies. Was he seriously suggesting that she live with him as his wife? What would it be like, seeing him every day, living with him, working with him, *sleeping* with him? Was she seriously considering it?

No, of course she wasn't! She would be crazy to commit herself to a perfect stranger, no matter how reassuring his face. She wouldn't even think about accepting.

'I presume that since you were planning to work in Jatipakan you didn't have any commitments for the next few weeks?' Gil said, when she didn't say anything.

'No, no commitments,' she said slowly. She *was* thinking about it, she realised in astonishment. 'I'm on my way to Australia, but I didn't have any definite date to arrive there.' Could that really be her, sitting there and calmly discussing pretending to be this man's wife, as if she had known him for years instead of a matter of minutes?

'Well, then.' Gil sat back and watched the emotions chasing over Deborah's transparent face. 'I'm not denying that it would suit me, but you'd be mad to turn down the offer.'

'I could always go to Parang,' she reminded him, feverishly trying to work out her options. 'It's probably not nearly as dangerous as you say it is.'

Gil shrugged. 'You could try, of course, but I wouldn't recommend it. Quite apart from anything else, if the authorities find you there without the proper papers, you'll be in big trouble.'

'I wouldn't have any papers if I came with you, either,' she pointed out.

'No, but I've some influence with the police in Terawati. I know them well through working with them on the scheme, and I could arrange a temporary permit for you to cover the three months. It would only cover the local area, of course, in case you felt like doing anything stupid like running away halfway through our agreement. I wouldn't have any hesitation in asking the police to let their colleagues in Parang know that you were wandering around illegally.' He paused. 'I could always do that this afternoon, too, if you insist on going to Parang on your own. For your own safety, of course,' he finished smoothly.

Deborah lifted her chin at the threat. 'That's not very fair!' There she had been thinking he knew about honour, too! He wasn't so honourable that he was above some blackmailing to get his own way!

'Life isn't very fair,' he said with brutal frankness. 'You're the one who put yourself in this situation after all. If you weren't so irresponsible, you wouldn't have to consider it.'

Deborah's brain was working frantically. If she refused his offer, she could end up spending the night in a police station, or on the street, or worse. And what would she do once she had got through the night? She could hardly stow away on the ferry to Jakarta, and her chances of finding a job teaching English in a town like Parang were remote, to say the least.

Or she could go with Gil Hamilton...

'You haven't left me with much of a choice, have you?' she accused him with a show of bravado as she played for time.

'You're lucky you've got a choice at all. I'm merely offering you the chance of a job that will solve your problems as well as mine.'

'All right.' Deborah ran her finger round the rim of her glass and took a deep breath to steady her nerves. 'Since we're talking in terms of a job, perhaps we'd better define exactly what my duties would be?'

'Helping in the office as required. Entertaining. In public, I'd expect you to convince everyone that you were indeed my wife.'

'And in private?' Deborah nerved herself to ask.

The light grey eyes bored into hers. 'If you're wondering if this is an elaborate charade to get you into bed, Deborah, you can put it out of your mind right now! I've had enough of women recently. They're a damned nuisance, either determined to distract you or unprepared to help you when you want them! My only interest at the moment is to get the new contract and get through the next few weeks with the minimum fuss, and I'm not going to have the time to seduce you, even if I did feel so inclined, which is, frankly, extremely unlikely.'

'Silver-tongued devil, aren't you?' Deborah said sourly.

Gil ignored that. 'The bungalows only have one bedroom each, so we'd have to share, but there are standard single beds. It shouldn't be too much of a problem to arrange some privacy at night without alerting everyone to the fact that we're not really married.'

'What if we don't get on?'

'I'll pay you a generous salary to make sure that we *do* get on,' he said flatly. 'But if you agree to this, Deborah, I don't want you changing your mind halfway. You go into this with your eyes wide open. I'm not prepared to look a fool with my supposedly new bride running away after a couple of weeks. Treat it like any other job. If you come, you come and do the job properly, but you'd better make up your mind fast. The bus is going to go any minute now.'

Deborah chewed her lip, glancing nervously over her shoulder at the passengers drifting towards the bus. She had to make a decision. She could take her chance alone in Parang, or she could take her chance with Gil.

Parang was a dangerous town, and in spite of her brave words about finding a job even Deborah's insouciance quailed at the prospect of surviving there with no money.

Gil might not be the most charming man in the world, but he was at least reassuringly British. In spite of his unnerving brusqueness, Deborah felt instinctively that she could trust him. He had said that he had no interest in her as a woman, and she believed him. She ought to be relieved instead of feeling obscurely piqued! He had made it abundantly clear that he had no interest in her other than as a purely business proposition, so it shouldn't be too hard to do as he said and pretend that it was just a rather unusual job. It wouldn't be too difficult to pretend in public; it might even be quite fun. And it would give her a chance to stay in Serok as she had wanted.

Deborah's natural buoyancy began to recover from the shock of Gil's extraordinary proposal. She had always wanted adventure, hadn't she? What would this be but an adventure? She ought to be seizing the opportunity with both hands instead of dithering around wondering just what it was about Gil that unsettled her and reassured her at the same time.

Behind her the driver climbed into his seat and started up the bus with a self-important roar. Deborah looked at him, and then back at Gil. It was now or never. She swallowed. 'All right,' she said in a rush. 'I'll do it.'

'Good.' Gil wasn't a man who wasted much time in effusive thanks, but he seemed to relax and for the first time it occurred to her that he might not have been as confident of her agreement as he had seemed.

'On one condition.'

He looked wary once more. 'What's that?'

'That you never, ever call me Debbie. I don't mind pretending to be your fiancée, but I can't bear having my name shortened,' she said firmly. 'I'm Deborah.'

For a moment she thought he would object but then quite suddenly the grim lines of his face relaxed into a disquietingly attractive smile. It warmed the grey eyes and curled the cool, unexpected mouth and, unprepared for the transformation, Deborah felt the breath dry in her throat. 'Very well,' he said. 'Deborah it is. Shall we shake on it?'

He held out his hand. Deborah took a deep breath and willed her heart to stop jumping around as if it had been kicked into action. Moistening her lips, she took his hand, and felt his fingers close about hers. His hand was hard, slightly callused, and his firm grip conveyed a jolting surge of competence. Her whole arm tingled as he released her hand, and she stared down at it as if expecting to see the imprint of his palm burnt against her skin.

What had she done? she thought in a renewed attack of panic. Had she really agreed to throw in her lot with a man who could make her shiver just by touching her hand?

With the minimum of fuss, Gil explained the situation to the bus driver and rescued her rucksack from its precarious position on the roof.

'Is this it?' he asked, looking down his nose. It was looking decidedly the worse for wear after months of travelling and Deborah wasn't surprised to see his look of distaste.

'This is it,' she confirmed, patting it affectionately. She and her rucksack had been through a lot together. 'I like to travel light.'

'Just as well, the way you look after your things,' Gil said acidly, but he picked it up and carried it over to the car.

With an excruciating grinding of gears, the bus pulled out on to the road, belching black exhaust. The driver gave Deborah a grin as he passed, and she smiled and waved back. The rucksack momentarily forgotten, she stood next to Gil and they watched the bus pick up speed as it headed downhill. The next moment it had disappeared round the bend to be swallowed up by the forest.

They listened to its roar, punctuated by the sound of changing gears, recede into the distance until the hot, humid silence settled about them like a blanket. An insect whirred frantically in the undergrowth and someone was clattering a wok in the kitchen shack, but otherwise all was quiet.

Deborah cleared her throat. 'Well, looks as if it's too late to change our minds now!'

'Yes.' Gil became brisk and practical once more. He frowned down at the rucksack. 'We'll have to hide this somehow. You can't turn up lugging one of these or you'll never convince anyone you're my wife. We don't want it to look as if you've just fallen off a bus, even if you have. I don't suppose you've got much in the way of smart clothes in here either?'

Deborah thought of her four T-shirts which always looked faintly grubby now, no matter how hard she scrubbed them. She had a pair of loose cotton trousers and an Indian cotton dress, but that was about as far as it went.

'I don't think you'd call them smart, no,' she said. 'Why don't I hide them all with the rucksack and we can pretend the airline lost my suitcase?'

'That would explain your not having any decent clothes,' Gil agreed. He looked at her with a critical eye. 'We're going to have to tidy you up before we get there. Nobody who saw you now could possibly believe that you were my wife!'

'What do you mean?' said Deborah, looking down at her jeans and red shirt. She had practically lived in her jeans, but they were looking a little ragged now and there was a sticky mark on her shirt where the little girl on the bus had wiped her hand. Deborah rubbed at it absently.

'You look a mess,' said Gil brutally. 'Have you got anything other than jeans in there?'

'A dress.'

'You'd better go and put it on.' Before she had time to protest, he had walked away to consult the owner of the restaurant, and Deborah was left to stare after him resentfully. Surely she didn't look that bad?

'He says you can change round the back,' said Gil, coming back. 'And wash your face while you're at it!'

Grumbling to herself, Deborah followed a waiter behind the restaurant, where he poured her a bowl of water from the well and left her inspecting her reflection in a tiny, cracked mirror with horror. No wonder Gil had been unimpressed! Her hair had come undone from its braid and was falling around her grubby face. She looked like a messy schoolgirl.

Her hands were as dirty as the rest of her, she thought ruefully, and scrubbed them as well as she could in the cold water before washing her face thoroughly and brushing out her long brown hair. It took ages to comb out the tangles, but at last it tumbled in soft waves over her shoulders. Imagining Gil fretting with impatience, Deborah changed quickly into her Indian dress. It was rather shapeless, hanging straight down to a dropped waist with two large pockets, but it was cool and comfortable and the cotton was a deep blue that matched her eyes. She smoothed it down a little nervously, wondering what Gil would think.

She made her way back to the front of the restaurant and looked around for Gil. He had evidently expected her to be some time, for he was sitting at one of the tables again, gazing down thoughtfully into a glass of coffee, but he looked up as if sensing her presence. For a moment he stared at her as if not recognising her.

'Good God!' He got to his feet without thinking as she came over to him. 'You look different.'

'I've let my hair down,' she said awkwardly. 'I usually tie it back because it's cooler, but I thought I might look more like a wife like this.' His silence was unnerving and she touched her hair with a nervous gesture. 'Will I do?' She twirled self-consciously before him. The blue cotton swirled about her long legs and the dark, glossy hair swung loose.

When he still didn't say anything, she stopped. He was probably comparing her to Debbie or the sultry Sylvie, and suddenly she felt plain and frumpy. She had never worried about clothes and was happy to pull on the first thing that came to hand in the morning, but for the first time ever she wished she had something nicer to wear. 'It's not very smart,' she said with a touch of defiance, 'but it's the best I can do, I'm afraid. At least it's clean.'

Gil cleared his throat. 'It's a great improvement.'

Well, she hadn't expected him to be the kind of man who was free with compliments, had she? Deborah squashed a feeling of illogical disappointment. It didn't matter what Gil thought about her. This was just a job.

His eyes still on her, he drained his coffee and dropped some money on the table. 'Come on,' he said. 'We've wasted enough time here. Let's go.'

Deborah adjusted the air-conditioning so that the cold air blew directly on to her face and relaxed back into her seat. She felt cocooned in luxury.

Blessed with a naturally breezy optimism that had seen her through many crises, Deborah felt her spirits rise. Here she was travelling back up the same road she had come down this morning on the bus, but what a difference between the two journeys! Then she had been tired and hot and uncomfortable; now she was cool and had a whole seat to herself. Then she had been facing the dismal prospect of leaving Serok, scraping by in Parang until the ferry came; now she could spend three months here and earn more than enough to continue with her travels. Things weren't ideal, of course. She didn't know anything about where she was going, she had no passport and to all intents and purposes she was utterly dependent on the man sitting next to her.

She stole a glance at Gil from under her lashes. His eyes were steady on the road ahead, his hands strong and competent on the steering-wheel. It was impossible to know what he was thinking. Deborah was struck again by the sense of a power kept under strict control. He might like to give the impression of cool reserve, but his mouth suggested a passion that might flare at any moment, a passion she was sure that he chose not to acknowledge. He was a study in contrasts, she thought, his deliberately understated appearance at odds with the quiet strength of his personality. Her first impression had been of a rather ordinary man, of intelligence and capability rather than obvious good looks; but he had a subtle magnetism about him that was as hard to deny as it was to explain, and the more she looked at him, the more she realised that he was in fact an unnervingly attractive man.

What would it be like sharing a room with him? Deborah felt an unsettling stir of awareness at the prospect and she looked away from Gil to stare out of the window. She had never been prudish. Out of necessity, she had often shared tents and hostel rooms with friends made on her travels, and there had never been any question of sex. They had just been making the best of things.

Why, then, should the thought of sleeping in the same room as Gil Hamilton make her shift uneasily in her seat? That would be making the best of things too. There would be no need for any embarrassing intimacy. It was just a job. They would have a bed each, and for all Gil was interested in her she might as well sleep behind a locked and bolted door.

CHAPTER THREE

UNTHINKINGLY, Deborah sighed.

'What's the matter?' Gil asked abruptly.

'Nothing. At least,' she improvised, 'I was just thinking that it might not be as easy as I thought to impersonate someone I know absolutely nothing about. What do I need to know about Debbie?' she asked, hoping that he wouldn't guess just how curious she was about his fiancée. 'Is she like me?'

'No,' said Gil with a certain dryness. 'You couldn't be more different. Debbie's quiet and pretty and sensible and feminine.'

Deborah looked affronted. 'I'm feminine!'

'You don't seem to worry very much about what you look like,' he said with another disparaging look. 'Debbie takes a lot of care over her appearance. She likes everything to be neat and tidy; it's one of the things that makes her such an efficient secretary.'

'She sounds very boring,' said Deborah, still smarting about not being feminine enough for him. She looked crossly out of the window at a vast clump of bamboo. The road was narrow and pot-holed, overhung by jungly vegetation which threatened at times to take it over completely. Everything still steamed gently after the morning's downpour and drops of rain trembled on the ends of the leaves.

'Debbie is not boring,' Gil said stiffly.

'Well, I hope I don't have to spend the next three months pretending to be exactly like her, that's all!' she said in a sulky voice.

'I should imagine you'd find that rather difficult,' he snapped back. 'I haven't told everyone the ins and outs of her character. I just said that she was a good secretary.'

Deborah shot him a puzzled look. She couldn't understand why a man with a mouth like that should pretend to be so lacking in passion. She didn't have the nerve to ask him, though. 'How did you meet?' she said instead.

'She worked as my secretary before Pascal and I went into partnership, so she understands why I have to be abroad so much. When I came out here, we agreed that it would be more sensible if she stayed in London. She works in the City now.'

Sensible! Deborah suppressed a sigh. Hadn't they ever heard of mad, impetuous flings? It sounded a strangely businesslike relationship. Was Gil really in love with Debbie, or were his feelings for her much deeper than he would admit? Deborah had always imagined that if she met someone she loved enough to spend the rest of her life with there would be no reason not to get married at once, but Debbie seemed to have viewed the matter in a quite different light. Gil had said that she wanted time to plan the wedding, but to Deborah's mind that was giving the wedding ceremony more importance than the bridegroom. Still, perhaps she was being unfair. Perhaps Debbie didn't want to be rushed into marriage.

'How long have you known each other?' she asked, trying not to sound as if she was prying.

'About three years.'

'Three years!' she echoed in amazement. Surely that was plenty of time to decide whether you wanted to be married or not? 'How long do you need to plan a wedding?'

'Not everyone shares your spontaneous approach to life,' he said acidly. 'Some people like to do things properly.'

'You can spend so much time worrying about doing something properly that you end up not doing it at all,' she pointed out, and his face shuttered.

'You can keep your philosophy to yourself. All I'm concerned about is that you do the job I'm paying you to do properly.'

Deborah was stung by an unreasonable jealousy at his defence of Debbie. It was Debbie who had let him down, after all! 'I'll do the best I can,' she said sullenly, 'but I don't have much background to go on. If anyone asks me, why didn't we get married before now, apart from the time it takes to choose the colour of the icing on a wedding cake?'

Gil shot her a look, but all he said was, 'Just say that the time never seemed right.'

'Whereas when you came back for this conference in London and wanted to get married at two days' notice, I leapt at the idea?' she suggested with some sarcasm.

Unexpectedly, the austere face gleamed with amusement. He didn't actually smile, but the cool curve of his mouth became more pronounced and the creases deepened at the edges of his eyes. 'Why not?' He glanced at her again and Deborah felt her heart do a slow somersault and land with an uncomfortable thud. 'It's not very convincing, I know, but you'll just have to tell them you couldn't keep your hands off me any longer!'

To her horror, Deborah felt a flush surge up her throat to stain her cheeks, but she forced herself to meet his eyes. 'Why don't you tell them *you* couldn't keep your hands off *me*?' she retorted bravely.

Gil gave his attention back to the road. 'I expect they'll see that for themselves,' he said.

Deborah looked uncertainly at the disconcerting almost-smile still lurking around his mouth, then tore her eyes away. 'Well,' she said with forced gaiety, studying the glove compartment while the memory of how his smile had changed his face simmered at the edge of her mind, 'now I know what I did, and how we met, but I don't know very much about my new husband.' Apart from the fact that he liked sensible girls and just looking at his mouth turned her bones to water. 'Can you give me a thumbnail sketch so I don't look too surprised if someone tells me you started out as a ballet dancer?'

'How did you guess?'

Forgetting her sudden shyness, Deborah gaped at him. 'You didn't!'

Gil gave in and grinned. 'No, I didn't. I have to admit that I've always been an engineer. When we were kids at the seaside, I used to build irrigation systems all over the beach. I never wanted to do anything else.'

It was unfair of him to grin like that just when she had got her heart under control. Deborah linked her hands in her lap and wished that he would go back to being cold and abrupt. It was easier on her pulse.

'You're lucky,' she said, amazed at how normal her voice sounded. 'I've never found out what I really want to do, apart from travel. I just have a good time, never having to commit myself to anything for very long.'

'I hope you'll be able to manage three months.'

'Oh, yes. In fact,' said Deborah, gazing reflectively out of the window, 'I'm looking forward to stopping in one place for a bit. That's why I tried to get the job in Jatipakan. I've been on the move for months now. I came overland,' she explained, ticking the countries off on her fingers. 'Turkey, Iran, Pakistan, Nepal, India. I had to fly from there to Thailand and then I came down through Malaysia and Singapore and now Indonesia.'

'Are you just drifting, or have you got an end in view?' Deborah was almost relieved to hear the disapproval edge back into Gil's voice.

'I'm on my way to Australia, as I said. I thought I'd try and work there.'

'And after that?'

'I don't know,' said Deborah, who never worried about the future.

'You'll have to settle down some time,' he said austerely.

She sighed. 'You sound like my father. My parents think that at twenty-four I should be thinking about getting married and having babies instead of gadding round the world.'

'You'd certainly be much safer,' he commented with some acidity. 'Why don't you get yourself a proper job?'

'I'm too young to settle down,' Deborah objected. 'I did a secretarial course after I left university, but it was only so I could get temporary jobs while I saved enough to travel. I spent a year in France as an au pair, but that was really hard work! It's easier to work as a temp for a few months, and then take off on a trip. I suppose I might want to stay in one place eventually, but in the meantime I'm having far too good a time to stop travelling.'

'It seems rather a haphazard way to go through life,' Gil commented, changing down a gear to go round a hairpin bend. The road was little more than a scar on the edge of the hillside now, and they emerged high above a breathtaking drop down into the valley. Deborah's pulse quickened. What a view! She had been right to come. Here she was, high in the jungle, on a rough, bumpy road with no idea where she was going, or what it was going to be like when she got there. She was living dangerously at last! The uncertain future and the unsettling presence of the man beside her gave an edge of excitement to her normally buoyant spirits.

'Maybe,' she said, 'but at least I'm here.' She gestured at the spectacular view. 'You can keep being sensible if it means staying at home and not seeing this!' Glancing defiantly at him, she added, 'I notice that you're here too! Perhaps you're not as sensible as you think you are!'

'I'm a professional,' he said dampeningly. 'Not only my future but the future of the people who work for me depends on my being here. I'm not here just to have a good time. I'm here to do a job.'

'So am I now,' Deborah pointed out with an innocent face.

'I hope you remember that,' he grunted.

'Don't worry, it can't be that difficult to act like a new bride. I'll just look smug. That should convince them.' She wriggled her shoulders into a more comfortable position in the luxurious upholstery. 'Who are "they" anyway? Will it just be Pascal and the dangerously distracting Sylvie or will there be anybody else around?'

Gil frowned at her flippant tone. 'There are about twenty of our engineers on site, but only two wives, Sylvie and Prim. She's a nurse, so she provides medical cover for the camp. It's not such a small community as it sounds, though, as the contractors have about four times as many expats in the camp and a number of them have wives out here as well.' His expression showed that he disapproved of such a lack of spartan spirit.

'I didn't realise you all lived in a camp,' said Deborah, wrinkling her nose. 'It doesn't sound very exotic. Can't we live in the town?'

'No, we can't. You'll live with me and not complain about it. The camp's not that bad, anyway. Terawati's just a small town, so we had to build a camp to accommodate all the engineers before we could even start work on the hydro-electric scheme. All the bungalows are the same, but there's a club with a swimming-pool and a bar. Terawati's just a couple of miles down the hill, and inevitably a few enterprising traders have set up *warungs*—stalls— around the camp. You might as well be in a town sometimes with all the noise from the boys pushing their carts along the roads! It's getting to be quite a thriving community.'

Deborah perked up. It didn't sound too bad. 'How much longer till we get there?'

'Another three hours at least.' The quiet, disturbing smile gleamed briefly once more. 'It's just as well you're so keen on the scenery, because you're going to see rather a lot of it!'

As the slow miles passed, Deborah lapsed into silence. The tarmac had quickly deteriorated once they had turned off the main Jatipakan road, and it was a rough, jolting trip in spite of the well-sprung vehicle. After a while, as Gil had warned, the scenery became increasingly monotonous. The road twisted endlessly up and down the hills, and the view round each bend was always exactly the same as the one before with the dense, snarled greenery pressing hypnotically on either side.

For Deborah, the journey became almost surreal, as if they were driving and driving without getting anywhere. Whenever the sense of oppressive growth threatened to become claustrophobic, she would look at Gil. His solid strength was infinitely reassuring, and her fears dissolved in the face of the clear, uncompromising lines of his body.

They had been going a couple of hours when it began to rain. The first splatter of drops like gunfire against the windscreen hardly had time to give warning before the black clouds unleashed a torrent of water. It fell in an impenetrable curtain around the car, pounding furiously on the metal roof, and involuntarily Deborah glanced upwards, half fearing to see the roof cave in beneath its savage onslaught. The noise was deafening, and she couldn't prevent a shiver. Every tropical downpour gripped her with the same queer mixture of pleasure and panic, of excitement and terror and awe at its ferocious power.

Gil muttered under his breath. He had slowed the car right down and was peering through the windscreen, leaning forward to try and see his way through the rain. The headlights were of little use, but the dashboard glowed eerily green, throwing his strongly defined face into relief, shadowing his eyes but catching the curve of mouth and the line of cheek.

Deborah's mouth dried in sudden, sharp awareness of him. Isolated by the crashing rain, trapped in this metal box, the space between them seemed absurdly small and electric with tension. She couldn't drag her eyes from his face, she couldn't stop wondering how his mouth would feel, what it would be like to reach out and touch the rough texture of his jaw or lay a hand on the lean length of his thigh.

Her mind burned with images so vivid that they shocked her. Terrified that her hands might move of their own accord, she linked them together in her lap and stared unseeingly down at them. She was concentrating so fiercely on subduing her imagination that she didn't notice when the drumming on the roof eventually stopped as suddenly as it had begun.

'Are you all right?' said Gil abruptly, switching off the windscreen wipers. The whirring of the air-conditioner sounded unnaturally loud in the vacuum the downpour had left behind. On either side of the road, the undergrowth had a battered, bedraggled look, its leaves still bent submissively beneath the sheer weight of the rain and dripping with exhaustion.

'I'm fine.' Deborah hoped her voice didn't sound as croaky to him as it did to her, and she searched feverishly for something to say to break the taut silence. 'How are we going to explain the fact that I'm not wearing a wedding-ring?' It was the first thing that came into her mind as she stared down at her bare fingers.

'Damn!' Gil swore quietly to himself. 'I hadn't thought of that. You're bound to have had a ring, aren't you? We'll just have to see if we can find something in Terawati.'

The brief tropical dusk was falling by the time they reached the town. They drove through the streets, weaving slowly between the seething crowds and the endless procession of street vendors who cried their wares as they pushed carts laden with everything from *sate* to plastic buckets and bamboo chairs. Their distinctive calls—cries, whistles, toots, bangings and ringings—rose above the cacophony and Deborah leant forward eagerly, forgetting her awkwardness in her enjoyment of the scene. It was so vibrant and colourful after the monotonous dark green of the jungle road.

Absorbed in what was going on around her, she was happy to wait in the car while Gil found a jeweller. Dusk seemed to be the busiest trading time of the day, and it wasn't long before he reappeared, pushing his way through the gang of little boys who had surrounded the car and were staring at a blissfully oblivious Deborah.

'It's not very traditional, but it's the nearest thing I could find,' he said. 'Here, give me your hand.'

Stupidly shy, Deborah held out her left hand and he slid a twisted ring of dull, beaten gold on to her third finger. She felt herself shiver at the brief touch of his fingers, and pulled her hand away quickly.

'It's too big, isn't it?' he said, eyeing it impersonally. 'Are you going to be able to keep it on?'

'It doesn't matter if it's a bit loose.' Deborah turned it wistfully round her finger. 'It's lovely.'

There was an odd, embarrassed silence, and then Gil turned away abruptly to switch on the ignition.

'You can keep it when you go, if you like.'

It was a brutal reminder of the temporary nature of their relationship. 'Sure you don't want to take the cost out of my wages?' said Deborah, her voice sharpened by illogical hurt at his callous attitude.

'That won't be necessary,' Gil said coldly. 'It's just part of the initial outlay you need to ensure the success of any project.'

They finished the journey in silence. A few miles up the bumpy road from Terawati, the lights of the camp were hidden in the forest, and the entrance seemed to Deborah to loom out of nowhere. It was fully dark by now, and she had a confused impression of neat, prefabricated bungalows laid out along unpaved streets, the starkness of their design softened by the abundant tropical growth. She saw palms drooping gracefully in the arc of the headlights, clusters of bougainvillaea and hibiscus, their bright colours hidden in the darkness, and when the car stopped and she opened the door the first thing that hit her was the heady fragrance of frangipani adrift in the hot, humid night.

'Oh, what a lovely smell!' she burst out. A frangipani tree stood by the path up to the darkened house, and she broke off a flower to hold it to her nose, letting the exotic scent envelop her. Its perfume was always more intense at night, and the white flowers gleamed through the darkness.

Still holding the flower, she turned and smiled at Gil in spontaneous delight.

'Deborah——'

He took a step towards her, but before she could learn what he was about to say the house behind them suddenly sprang into a blaze of light. Startled, they both swung round to see a crowd of people who had materialised as if by magic on the veranda, all grinning down at them indulgently.

'Surprise!' they cried.

In any other circumstances, Deborah would have found Gil's appalled expression funny. If they had been a genuine couple, she would have been touched that Gil's colleagues had gone to the trouble of welcoming them with a party to celebrate their marriage. As it was, her heart sank at the prospect. 'Oh, dear,' she said.

Gil's comment was pithier, and fortunately audible only to her as a ragged cheer went up from the veranda. Forcing a smile, he took her arm and moved forward into the light.

'Do you really think we can get away with this?' Deborah whispered in sudden panic, trying to hang back, but Gil pulled her inexorably with him.

'There's only one way to find out.'

Someone broke into a cheerful if tuneless whistle of the Wedding March as they climbed the steps to the veranda with identically fixed smiles, and now

Deborah was glad of Gil's reassuringly firm grip. In spite of the suffocating heat, his hand was cool. As they were swallowed up in a babel of congratulations, her strongest impression was of his fingers burning an imprint into the soft skin of her inner arm.

'Gil!' A stocky man pushed his way to the front and pumped Gil's hand. He was dark with an ugly, swarthy face that was somehow rather attractive. 'Welcome back!'

'Thank you.' Next to him, Gil looked even cooler and more austere than usual, but his smile was natural as he turned to introduce him to Deborah. 'My partner, Pascal Douviers. Pascal, this is...' there was a momentary hesitation before he finished easily enough '...my wife.'

Pascal studied Deborah with frank interest. 'Welcome at last, Debbie!' His warm brown eyes held a good deal of charm.

'Deborah,' she corrected firmly, and held out her hand, but he brushed it aside and insisted on kissing her on both cheeks in the French manner. 'Charming!' he said to Gil with Gallic appreciation. 'Very natural and English! You have good taste, my friend!' Then he turned back to Deborah. 'We are all so pleased to see you here, Deborah. Gil is always work, work, work, but now he has something much nicer to think about! Now you must come and meet Sylvie. I know she is looking forward to meeting you very much.'

From what she had heard about Sylvie, Deborah rather doubted it, but she never had a chance to make her polite reply. Gil's fingers tightened warningly around her arm and she turned her head to see the crowd clearing to let a stunningly attractive woman through.

Deborah wouldn't have needed the pressure of Gil's fingers to know that this was Sylvie. She had exotically pale skin with darkly slanting eyes and a bruised, discontented-looking mouth. Her black hair was cut short to emphasise the exquisite bone-structure and she walked up to Gil with a sinuous, self-consciously feline grace.

Ignoring Deborah, she put her hands on his shoulders and kissed him on both cheeks, but whereas Pascal's salutation had been charming Sylvie somehow managed to invest the same gesture with unbearable intimacy.

'We have missed you, Gil,' she said in a husky voice. Pronouncing it *Geel*, she made his name sound like a caress, and Deborah's eyes narrowed. So this was Sylvie! It was easy to see why Gil would have found her difficult to discourage, but for the first time Deborah wondered how hard he had tried. There was a smoulderingly seductive quality about the Frenchwoman that any man would find hard to resist.

Glancing at Gil, she saw that he was carefully expressionless. 'I'd like you to meet my wife, Sylvie,' he said.

Sylvie's eyes swept over Deborah, who knew with feminine instinct that no detail of her face, figure or dress had escaped her contemptuous scrutiny. 'So, this is little Debbie!'

'Not so little,' said Deborah, who was just as tall as Sylvie, but felt like an enormous, unsophisticated lump next to her. 'And my name's Deborah, not Debbie.'

'But Gil always talks about you as Debbie!'

'Not any more, he doesn't.'

They eyed each other with mutual dislike as Gil and Pascal became quickly involved in a discussion about how the project had progressed in Gil's absence.

'It is very good of you to come out to Indonesia at such short notice to help Gil in the office,' Sylvie went on condescendingly. She had obviously decided that Gil's only possible interest in her could be as a typist.

'It's not very hard to be with the man you love,' Deborah said sweetly. She leant her cheek winsomely against Gil's shoulder, and felt him stiffen in surprise. 'Not when you've been engaged as long as we have.' She might as well make sure that Sylvie knew her claim on Gil supposedly went back a long time. 'Besides, I'll be helping Gil in more than just the office, won't I, darling?'

At her tug, Gil turned from Pascal to look down at her warily. 'I was just telling Sylvie how wonderful it will be to be together all the time at last,' she explained. 'It's been awful spending all these years apart, hasn't it?'

'Awful,' Gil agreed woodenly, obviously taken aback at the spirit with which Deborah was entering into her part.

'But we're going to make up for it now that we can spend all day——' she lowered her lashes coyly '—and all night together.'

She saw with some satisfaction that Sylvie was looking decidedly sour. Gil's expression was harder to read but a muscle beat insistently in his cheek.

'It's a shame that you have not had time for honeymoon,' Pascal intervened. 'Poor Deborah, being put straight to work!'

'I don't mind,' said Deborah, assuming a virtuous expression. 'As long as I'm with Gil, I don't care where I am!' She allowed herself a smug look at Sylvie, who glared back.

Gil evidently decided that it was time he took charge of the conversation. 'There's so much work to do here that we've decided to wait. I've only got another three months, and then we can have a really good holiday without any pressure.'

'It's not a bad idea,' said Pascal. 'At least then we'll know if we have the new contract or not. Have you decided where you'll go yet?'

'Australia,' said Deborah, at the same time as Gil said,

'Bali,' and they looked at each other in consternation.

Sylvie's glance was speculative. 'You don't sound very sure!'

'We're stopping over in Bali on our way to Australia,' Gil said smoothly. 'Aren't we, darling?' he added, taking a leaf out of Deborah's book.

'I can't wait!' Deborah fluttered her eyelashes prettily, wondered if she would risk a kiss on Gil's cheek and decided she didn't dare.

'Pascal!' Sylvie said sharply. 'We mustn't monopolise Deborah. Everyone wants to meet her. Why don't you introduce her around?'

'Of course!' Pascal offered Deborah his arm gallantly and she could hardly refuse to go with him. 'I am neglecting my duties as host! This is Gil's house—your house, too, now—but as I invited everyone here to surprise you I suppose I am the host,' he explained. 'You know how reserved Gil is! He would never think of giving a party for himself, but we all wanted to celebrate his wedding. All the engineers have a lot of respect for him, and, more than that, they like him. He can be hard, but he's always fair. He's a good man to work for.'

'How long have you been partners?' Deborah asked, too interested in finding out more about the uncommunicative Gil to remember that she ought to be expected to know about his career.

Pascal didn't seem to notice anything odd about her question. 'Just eighteen months, but we have come a long way in that time. It was a risk, setting up as European partners, but it has worked out very well. If we get this new project, our future is assured. And it is largely thanks to Gil, I have to admit it.' He poured her some champagne and handed her the glass, toasting her silently as he continued. 'I am a good engineer, yes, even a brilliant designer, but Gil is the force behind our partnership. What a negotiator that man is! What an administrator!' Pascal became more and more French as he waxed eloquent. 'Without him, my designs would never become reality.'

'You must be good friends,' said Deborah, taking a cautious sip of her champagne and reflecting that it was the last thing she had expected to be drinking that night when she had set out from Jatipakan—was it really only that morning?

'Yes, we are good friends, and good colleagues.' Pascal glanced over to where Gil stood, still with Sylvie. She had her hand on his arm and was talking to him in a low, intimate voice. 'I would not want anything to come between us.' The ugly, attractive face was suddenly serious as his eyes rested on his wife. 'I am glad you are here,' he went on, summoning a smile as he turned back to Deborah. 'You will be good for Gil, good for all of us.' His eyes slid back to Sylvie and he repeated himself absently. 'Yes, I am very glad you are here.'

CHAPTER FOUR

DEBORAH was soon swept up into a round of introductions. The party had evidently been in full swing before they'd arrived, and she felt a little guilty at her deception in the face of such a friendly welcome. It seemed that Sylvie was the only person not delighted to meet her.

People kept thrusting glasses of champagne into her hand, and after a while Deborah began to enjoy herself. She had always loved meeting new people and since she had agreed to this strange arrangement with Gil she might as well make the most of it.

Every now and then she would catch a glimpse of Gil through the crowd. He was a steady rock in the midst of all the boisterous excitement, a calm, cool, controlled pivot around which the party swung. He never looked in her direction, and Deborah would take another swig of champagne, obscurely piqued.

He ought to show some interest in his supposed new bride, surely, instead of allowing Sylvie to monopolise him? The Frenchwoman always seemed to be hanging around him, leaning towards him, laughing a deep, throaty laugh that grated up and down Deborah's spine.

Deborah scintillated in response, keeping the group around her convulsed with laughter as she described imaginary incidents in her relationship with Gil. She would show him that others might not find her quite as uninteresting as he obviously did! She might not have a sultry laugh or a way of looking suggestive just by sipping a glass of champagne, but at least she remembered what she was doing here. Gil was the one who had gone on and on about the importance of convincing everyone that she really was his wife, but no one would have guessed from the way he was ignoring her!

Suddenly Deborah found herself dragged ruthlessly aside by a short, curvaceous girl with a riot of curls and naughty brown eyes who introduced herself as Prim.

'Primrose when I'm in trouble,' she explained. 'But I can't bear it, so I always shorten it to Prim. I've been dying to meet you,' she went on. 'I couldn't imagine what sort of girl Gil would marry! He's always been so reserved. Not exactly aloof but sort of...' She screwed up her face, searching for the right word.

'Self-contained?' suggested Deborah, catching sight of him out of the corner of her eye. He was talking to a group of younger men and although he was relaxed and smiling the subtle air of authority was obvious even from the other side of the room. Sylvie was there too, of course. Why didn't he tell her to go away and leave him alone?

'That's it exactly! Self-contained.' Prim sighed. 'I expect that's what makes him so attractive. He's so restrained, and I can never put my finger on why he should be so gorgeous at the same time. Do you know what I mean?'

Deborah glanced at Gil again. Strange that every angle of his face should already be so familiar. 'Yes, I know what you mean.'

'I must say, it's nice to see Gil smitten at last,' Prim said with a satisfied air.

'Smitten?' Deborah sent Sylvie a dark look. Was it obvious to everyone?

'I always thought he'd be rather a cool husband,' Prim said apologetically. 'It was just the way he used to talk about you. He'd talk about how efficient you were, but never about how blue your eyes were.'

That was hardly surprising, Deborah reflected, as the other girl leant forward confidentially. 'To tell you the truth, Deborah, I was rather dreading your coming. From what Gil said, I imagined you as being terribly smart and we'd all have to mind our "p"s and "q"s, but I can see now that you're not like that at all.'

Deborah had to laugh. Nothing could be further from the truth. It was comforting to know that she wasn't the only one who had decided that Debbie sounded a dead bore. 'I'm not like that at all,' she reassured Prim. 'Gil must have been joking if he gave you that impression.'

'He certainly had us all convinced,' said Prim, a little puzzled. 'Perhaps he wanted to keep you all to himself. It must be a case of attraction of opposites. Funny, it always gets them in the end, and when a man like Gil falls he falls heavily!'

Had he fallen more heavily than he wanted to admit for Sylvie? Deborah wondered glumly. Was she just here to disguise his feelings for the other woman?

Prim was chattering on. 'If it weren't for the fact that I'm madly in love with Michael, I'd be quite envious of you. He obviously adores you.'

'He does?' Deborah said stupidly, before she remembered that she shouldn't sound so astonished at the idea.

Prim looked at her a little strangely. 'He's still trying to be the same cool old Gil, but he can't take his eyes off you. Whenever he thinks no one's watching, he looks round for you.'

'He *does*?' said Deborah again, glancing involuntarily over her shoulder, and this time Gil did look up. Across the room, their eyes met with an unexpected jolt of electricity that stopped Deborah's heart and then kicked it back into thudding life. The colour flamed in her cheeks, and she turned quickly back to Prim.

'See what I mean?' Prim sighed sentimentally. 'I think it's so romantic to see the way you both look at each other when you think the other's not watching. I can't think why two people so much in love should wait so long to get married! The wedding must have been lovely,' she went on. 'I'd love to see your photos.'

Deborah stared at her in consternation. Everyone had a photo of their wedding! How was she going to explain the absence of theirs?

To her relief, she felt Gil approach. She couldn't see him coming up behind her, but her spine tingled and she knew instantly that he was there.

'I've brought you some more champagne,' he said in his cool way, taking the empty glass from her hand and replacing it with a full one. For once he wasn't shadowed by Sylvie.

Deborah's pulse leapt at the merest brush of his fingers, and she said on a half-gasp, 'Prim was just asking about our wedding photos.'

There was a tiny pause. 'Didn't Deborah tell you?' Gil said easily. 'I'm afraid we had a bit of a disaster on the way out and the airline lost her suitcase.'

'All the photos were in there,' Deborah said, seizing eagerly on his cue.

'Oh, what a shame!' cried Prim. 'Never mind, you'll be able to get some new ones made up from the negatives. I don't suppose you could organise a very big wedding at such short notice?'

'It was fun, though, wasn't it, Gil?' said Deborah, remembering the extravagant way she had described their mythical wedding after seeing Sylvie whisper in Gil's ear.

'So Roger's just been telling me.' There was no mistaking the edge to his voice. 'I gather you described it to him in vivid detail. He was quite surprised when he overheard me telling Michael what a quiet wedding it was.'

Deborah hung her head guiltily. Perhaps she *had* got a bit carried away, but Roger had laughed so much at her imaginative description that it had been impossible to avoid embellishing her account with even more amusing anecdotes.

'I told Roger that you were prone to wild fits of exaggeration,' Gil added with a warning look that succeeded only in rousing Deborah's defiance.

Prim looked from one to another a little curiously. 'You were lucky to arrange a reception in a week,' she said mildly. 'Did you have it at a hotel or at home?'

Deborah opened her mouth to reply but Gil got in first. 'In a hotel,' he said briefly, giving Prim no encouragement to carry on asking questions; but she was not to be deterred.

'What was your dress like, Deborah?'

Feeling Gil sigh beside her, Deborah seized on her chance. Let him deny this if he dared! As a child she had had a picture of Cinderella marrying Prince Charming, and she described it now to a wide-eyed Prim in convincing detail. 'It had a long, full underskirt, and scalloped silk over it with pearls embroidered on it—it was so pretty!' Gil was looking appalled, she noted with satisfaction. For a moment she toyed with the idea of dressing him in Prince Charming's satin breeches and ruffled shirt, but rejected it reluctantly. She didn't want to push him too far. 'It was a sort of seventeenth-century effect, you know,' she went on confidingly to Prim, but with one eye on Gil's expression. 'With ruffles of lace around the neckline and at the elbows. And I had a veil, of course, a long one with a train, and fresh flowers in my hair.'

'It sounds lovely,' Prim sighed and Deborah was unable to resist sending Gil a provocative look.

'Gil said I looked *beautiful*, didn't you, darling?' she pretended to reminisce, with just the right degree of smugness.

Gil looked boot-faced. 'You looked very nice,' he said between clenched teeth.

'I'm amazed you managed to get it made up in time,' Prim commented. 'Usually it takes months.'

'Oh, I've had it ready for ages,' said Deborah, who was thoroughly enjoying herself. 'I've just been waiting for Gil to stop prevaricating and name the day!'

A nerve was twitching in Gil's jaw. 'You didn't want to give up your job either, if you remember, *darling*.' His light eyes held a warning, but Deborah had had enough champagne not to care. She assumed a mournful expression.

'I'd have given it up for you years ago if you'd really wanted me to.'

As if sensing the tension, Prim changed the subject. 'What about your other stuff, Deborah? Did you lose all your clothes as well as the photos?'

'I'm afraid so.' Deborah held her arms away from her body and looked down at her blue dress ruefully. 'I've only got what I stand up in.'

'You poor thing! I can lend you whatever you need, of course, but you're so much slimmer than me, my clothes will probably hang off you.' Prim eyed Deborah's slender figure enviously. 'Honestly, you never know what these airlines are going to do with your luggage nowadays!'

'It's amazing how careless some people are when it comes to bags,' Gil said with something of a snap, and Deborah poked the tip of her tongue out at him before Prim could see.

'Never mind, it'll be a good excuse for Gil to buy you some new clothes.'

Prim winked at Deborah, who said breezily, 'Oh, I don't mind. I don't care what I wear, as long as it's comfortable.'

'Really?' Prim looked surprised. 'I thought you told me she was always turned out immaculately, Gil?'

'She *used* to be,' he said. 'But then she had that accident.' He shook his head sadly, and Deborah knew that he was getting his own back. 'She's never been quite the same since.'

'Oh, I didn't know.' Prim turned to Deborah with a nurse's concern. 'I'm so sorry. Were you badly hurt?'

'No,' said Deborah, with a frosty glance at Gil. 'It was just a bump. I've always been exactly the same.' She beckoned Prim closer with an ingenuous air. 'The truth is that Gil has always thought of me as perfect. He's been abroad so much that I think he's built up this image of me in his mind, and now I'm afraid it's a bit of a shock to find out that I'm not quite the superwoman he thought I was.'

Gil had heard enough. 'Would you excuse us a minute, Prim?' he said, taking Deborah's wrist in a hard grasp. She could sense his anger, but the only outward signs of it were the rigid set of his jaw and the muscle beating in his cheek. 'I just need a quick word with Deborah.'

Without waiting for Prim's reply, he began to drag her out of the crush, clearly intent on giving her a piece of his mind. Deborah, unrepentant, kept a bright smile pinned to her face. He might have forgotten that they were supposed to be blissfully happy newly-weds, but she hadn't!

'There you are, Gil!' Pascal bore down on them before Gil had reached the door. 'I've been looking for you and your lovely bride everywhere!'

'I just wanted a private word with Deborah.' Gil gritted his teeth at being balked so near to his goal.

'I know, *mon ami*!' Pascal clapped him on the shoulder with a meaningful wink. 'You two want to be alone. Don't worry, we will all go in just a minute, but first I want to propose a toast.' He raised his voice, shouting above the hubbub of conversation, 'Ladies and gentlemen! Silence, if you please!'

Gil muttered beneath his breath as the chatter died away obediently and expectant faces turned towards them, but Pascal was clearing his throat and didn't hear.

'Gil and Deborah got married just three days ago, and they've come straight back to join us in order to make sure that we have the best possible chance of winning the contract for the second stage of the Tanah Terawati scheme. You can't ask for more dedication than that, but I don't think any of us would have expected anything else of Gil, who has always put the interests of those who work for him above his own.'

There was a rumble of 'Hear! Hear!' and Pascal turned to Deborah. 'I have to confess that I used to wonder if Gil was married to his work, but now that I have seen the delightful bride he has chosen I can see that the job will be the last thing on his mind when he goes home at night!' Everyone laughed, and Deborah blushed becomingly. 'I know that everyone here would like to join me in wishing you both many, many years of happiness together.'

'Hear! Hear!' said everyone again.

'So I'd like you all to raise your glasses and drink to . . . Gil and Deborah!'

There was a good-natured chorus of 'Gil and Deborah!' and 'Gil and Debbie!' from those who hadn't yet heard about the change of name.

Deborah avoided Gil's eye. He was still gripping her wrist, and she wondered what they would all say if he told them they were only planning to stay 'married' for three months, and probably a lot less if she didn't behave better! Surely he was regretting that he had ever embarked on this pretence?

Of course, he had to pretend that it was for real. 'Thank you all very much,' he said, when he could make himself heard. 'I know that Deborah appreciates such a warm welcome as much as I do.'

Very cool, very understated, very Gil. His colleagues were obviously used to his style, for they laughed and a camera flashed so close that Deborah blinked.

'Give her a kiss!' someone shouted from the back of the crowd, and another voice took up the call. 'Yes, a kiss for the camera! Come on, Gil, kiss the bride!'

Deborah's bright bride's smile froze. Caught unawares, Gil's fingers slackened around her wrist and she turned to look up at him as if her head were pulled by some invisible string, expecting to see the same appalled look that she was sure was reflected in her own blue eyes.

His face was carefully expressionless, his eyes very light and clear against his tan.

'Kiss the bride!'

'Come on, Gil, she's your wife now!'

Deborah swallowed. She didn't see any way they could get out of it, and evidently Gil didn't either, because his fingers tightened again on her wrist and he drew her towards him almost roughly.

After that, everything seemed to happen in slow motion. To Deborah, the cheerful whistles and laughter faded away as Gil lifted his other hand and pushed the tumbling hair away from her face. His fingers burned against her cheek and then slid to cup her chin while the hand that held her wrist pulled her closer.

Deborah found that she was trembling. Her heart was thudding against her ribs, her pulse beating insistently with some unknown need as slowly, very slowly, he bent his head.

Even so, when his mouth touched hers, she was unprepared for the jolt of excitement that surged through her, and she gave a tiny gasp, parting her lips instinctively.

His kiss was hard and almost fierce, as if he wanted to punish her, and it would have been over swiftly if something totally unexpected hadn't leapt into life between them just as the pressure of his lips lessened and he was about to lift his head. It was an electrifying thrill of recognition, a rocketing excitement that shook them off balance and left them helpless to resist.

Dimly, Deborah was aware that they should pull away, that they should carry on smiling and being polite, but her body seemed to have acquired a will of its own, and her lips moved against Gil's with growing urgency. His mouth was insistent, exciting, *warm*. How could she ever have thought it would be cool?

Gil was as unprepared as she, Deborah was sure. She knew he wanted to break away, but his lips were bewitched, caught in a spell they wove themselves. The hand on her wrist slid up her bare arm and cupped the other side of her face, his thumbs caressing her soft skin. She murmured low in her throat in response and her own hands clutched at his shirt as if it were an anchor against the exhilaration spinning her senses into a vortex of passion.

In the end, Gil had to jerk his head away with a physical effort before they could break the kiss. Deborah's eyes were dazed and blue as she blinked at the grinning crowd and tried desperately to force herself back to reality. Had that really been her, clinging to Gil—*Gil*!—and kissing him as if she wanted him and needed him and loved him?

Risking a glance at him, she saw that he looked perfectly composed. The striking light eyes were shuttered and told her nothing.

It had only been a kiss, after all. A kiss for the camera, and then it was done.

She was still standing as if rooted to the spot, staring down at her sandals. The stitching on one of the straps was coming apart, she noticed irrelevantly. Her knees felt ridiculously weak and she was afraid that if she moved at all she would simply collapse. Convinced that everyone must be able to tell from her face that it was the first time Gil had kissed her and that they must all be sniggering at its devastating effect, she forced herself to look up. Nobody was pointing or laughing. They all had the happily satisfied look of successful matchmakers. Half incredulous, her gaze moved round the room until she came to a pair of dark eyes that looked anything but happy or satisfied.

Sylvie stared back at her malevolently, and Deborah tilted her chin in instinctive challenge. She wouldn't give Sylvie the satisfaction of knowing that Gil had had to go to the lengths of buying a strange girl to protect himself from her. Knowing that Sylvie would hate it, Deborah smiled straight at her and then moved closer to Gil to take his hand possessively.

He looked down at their linked hands, but he didn't pull away as she half suspected he might. He didn't meet her eyes, either, but his fingers tightened briefly around hers.

Suddenly Prim was waving a scarf in front of her face.

'What's that for?' Deborah asked blankly.

'It's a blindfold. We've all clubbed together to buy you a wedding present, but it's too big to wrap and we want it to be a surprise.'

Not a crystal decanter, then. Deborah was beginning to wish they would all go away and leave her alone with Gil. At least then she wouldn't have to pretend. Still, she suffered herself to be blindfolded along with an equally resigned Gil, and led with much laughter and jostling into another room.

'Here we are!' she heard Pascal say. 'The present is from all of us, Gil. We couldn't think what to give you that you could carry easily around the world with you, so we decided to try and make your last three months here as nice as possible. You may not have had a honeymoon yet, but at least at night you can feel like newly-weds. We had it made specially for you,' he added proudly. 'OK, take off the blindfolds now!'

The scarf fell from Deborah's eyes and she blinked to clear her vision. She was standing facing Gil, with everyone crowding round them, grinning in expectation of their delight.

Gil was staring down at what stood between them, with no expression on his face at all, and Deborah was seized with sudden foreboding as she followed his gaze downwards.

It was an enormous double bed.

'Thank God that's over!' Gil came back after firmly ushering the last of their guests out and threw himself down in one of the chairs with an exasperated sigh.

Deborah was wandering rather nervously around the room, pretending to inspect it for the first time. There was little enough to inspect: some rattan chairs and a sofa, covered with plain cushions, a desk with neat piles of reports, a few books arranged in an orderly fashion on shelves and, at the far end of the room, a dining table whose chairs were placed around it with military precision. Above, two ceiling fans creaked as they slapped lethargically at the hot air.

Having longed for everyone to leave, Deborah now wished they hadn't. Her mood kept swinging from champagne-induced euphoria to edgy apprehension whenever she allowed herself to think about Gil's kiss and the prospect of climbing into the same bed with him. His expression wasn't designed to put her at her ease, either. His jaw was clenched with suppressed anger, and the eyes that followed her around the room were distinctly unfriendly.

Unable to bear the silence any longer, Deborah cleared her throat. 'I think everyone believed we were married, anyway.'

'Only until they start comparing notes,' Gil snapped. 'What the hell did you think you were playing at with all those ridiculous stories?'

'I was playing at being your wife.' Deborah picked up a bowl of peanuts from the coffee-table and finished them off with a show of bravado. 'I thought that's what you were paying me for?'

'I'm not paying you to make up a lot of damn fool stories about me!' Gil got to his feet as if too angry to sit still and began clearing up the debris from the party. 'I even had to pretend I knew what Emily Watts was talking about when she told me how I proposed to you on Brighton beach in the pouring rain!' The glasses clinked in protest as he loaded them aggressively on to a tray.

'It was the beach at Bamburgh,' Deborah corrected him. 'It's beautiful there. I told her that we drank a bottle of champagne under an umbrella. I thought I'd better make it sound romantic.'

'Romantic? What's romantic about being cold and wet and uncomfortable?'

'But Gil, remember how in love we were!'

Gil sent her a look of acute dislike. 'I'm beginning to think I must have been mad to get involved with you! The idea was that you should pretend to be Debbie, if you remember,' he added sarcastically. 'And it's extremely unlikely that either Debbie or I would have found it romantic with the wind howling off the North Sea in the middle of winter!'

'You probably proposed by sending each other memos promising to be eternally sensible,' retorted Deborah. She sat down on the sofa, put the bowl she had finished aside and applied herself to what remained of the nuts in another. 'Anyway,' she went on indistinctly, 'I had to make up something. I didn't have much information about Debbie to work on. All you told me was that she was smart and efficient, but people don't want to know how fast you can type. They wanted to know how we met, what you're really like, what the wedding was like, that kind of thing.'

'You didn't need to go into quite such extravagant detail!'

'Well, at least I behaved like a new bride,' said Deborah sulkily.

'Oh, is that what you were supposed to be like?' Gil said in a cutting voice. 'You could have fooled me! I got the impression of a stand-up comedienne or part of a circus troupe, certainly not a new bride. God knows what everybody else thought!'

'They probably thought I was being brave about the fact that my husband spent the whole evening being pawed by another woman!'

'What do you mean by that?' he said with dangerous calm.

'I thought you wanted to discourage Sylvie,' she accused him. 'It didn't look very discouraging the way you let her hang round like that! She was all over you. "Ah've meest you, Geel."' She mimicked Sylvie's accent with wicked accuracy. 'You weren't exactly beating her off, were you?'

Gil's face darkened. 'Look, I've told you, Deborah! I don't want to risk any kind of scene.

If I made it clear to Sylvie that I didn't want anything to do with her, she's the kind of woman who would make trouble by going to Pascal and claiming that I'd tried to seduce her.'

'Sure. And in the meantime it's not too awful having her pressing up against you and whispering sweet nothings in your ear in that sexy French way she has!' Deborah banged the bowl back on the coffee-table, unsure of why she felt so cross. 'Pascal's not a fool, anyway. She doesn't make any secret of what she feels for you!'

'That is precisely why I brought you here,' said Gil in an icy tone. 'I thought that you would have the sense to stay by me and keep quiet so that she didn't have an opportunity to "hang round" me, as you put it, but no! You bounced around the room, making up outrageous stories that completely contradicted what I was saying, and blatantly flirting with all the men! Hardly the behaviour of a new bride!'

'I wasn't flirting!' she protested. 'I assumed you'd want me to be nice to everyone.'

'There's a difference between being nice and making an exhibition of yourself! I got sick of people coming up to me and telling me what fun you were. Fun!' Gil snorted incredulously. 'More like a nightmare! "You thought I looked beautiful, didn't you, darling?"' It was his turn to mimic her savagely. 'What on earth made you say something like that?'

'It's the kind of thing brides say,' said Deborah, unrepentant. 'I know, I've heard them. And I bet Debbie would have said it!'

'Debbie would *not* have said it!' Gil's voice rose to a shout before he recovered himself. He glowered at Deborah, his jaw working in frustration. 'Debbie would have been quiet and sensible. She'd have managed to be pleasant to everyone without making them feel they were taking part in a sideshow, and Sylvie would have recognised at once that she stood no chance at all against her.'

'If Debbie's so marvellous, why isn't she here?' Deborah asked nastily. 'This was your idea, not mine. I could be halfway to Jakarta by now!'

'You could be languishing in some black hole in Parang without any way to get out! I suggest you remember that next time you feel like making up any more frivolous stories about me. I won't be paying you a penny until you start behaving yourself and remembering what you came here to do!'

CHAPTER FIVE

LEAVING Deborah fuming, Gil went outside to fetch their bags from the car. 'You'd better hide this,' he said, dropping her rucksack in the bedroom. 'I suggest you take out anything you might need and put the rest at the back of the wardrobe.'

Since she had claimed not to have any clothes, the only things Deborah could think were worth keeping out were her toothbrush, a sarong and her swimming-costume. The rest would be bundled away like a guilty secret.

Gil unpacked his suitcase with precise, economical gestures. Deborah watched him from under her lashes as she crouched down by her rucksack, the thick hair falling forward to hide her face. The double bed lurked at the edge of her vision. She tried to ignore it, but it refused to go away, mocking her with the image of sharing it with Gil, and the bravado that had buoyed her up during their argument began to drain slowly away.

She couldn't spin out her 'unpacking' any longer. Pushing her rucksack to the back of the cupboard, she got to her feet and went to perch on the edge of the bed with the vague thought that it might become less alarming if she confronted it directly.

'What are we going to do about the bed?'

'What do you expect me to do about it?' he replied irritably, slamming a drawer full of shirts shut. 'I can hardly go out and say that my wife refused to sleep with me, could we have our single beds back, please, can I? We'll just have to make the best of it. It's big enough for two, and I expect I'll be able to keep my hands off you.'

He was a pig, Deborah thought later, remembering his comment as she brushed her teeth crossly in the neat bathroom. A horrible, hateful pig! No wonder Debbie hadn't wanted to marry him! If he was half as unpleasant to Sylvie as he was to her, she would soon go off him! Why was she so keen on him anyway? It wasn't as if he was *that* attractive. He might have eyes that sent a shiver down her spine and an unnerving smile, but it didn't make him any less rude and unfeeling. It would serve him right if she *did* slip away to Parang in the night.

Here, Deborah's resolve faltered. She wouldn't put it past him to put the police on to her, and although they would get on to the British Embassy the wait might not be a pleasant one. And all the Embassy would do would be to get her parents to send enough money for her ticket and put her on the first plane home. Her parents couldn't afford that, and even if they could she wouldn't ask them. She had told them she could cope on her own, and that was what she was going to have to do.

No, she was better off here, in spite of Gil Hamilton. With the exception of Sylvie, everyone seemed very friendly, and there were worse ways of earning enough money to continue her travels. So what if it meant sharing a bed with Gil? It didn't bother her!

Tying her sarong securely under her arms, she marched back into the bedroom in a determined mood. Gil was already in bed. She could see his outline beneath the mosquito net. He lay on his back with his hands under his head. A single bedside lamp cast a dim glow, giving the powerful arms and solid chest a sculptured effect. The single sheet was drawn up above his waist, stirring slightly in the breeze from the overhead fan. Deborah wanted to know whether he wore anything underneath, but didn't dare to ask.

Glad of the subdued light, she went over to the bed. It dipped and creaked as she lifted the mosquito net and slipped beneath it. Taking a deep breath, she swung her legs up and leant back against her pillow. She lay stiffly at the very edge, terrified to move in case she rolled up against Gil.

'Why are you so nervous?' said Gil, leaning up on one elbow to switch off the lamp. The sudden darkness was loud with the frenzied whirring of insects outside, punctuated by the hypnotic slap-slap of the ceiling fan. Deborah could smell the frangipani drifting in through the wire mesh over the window.

'I'm not in the slightest bit nervous,' she said coldly.

'You mean you take sleeping with strange men in your stride?'

'When you're travelling, you often have to share rooms with strangers. It's just a matter of practicality.' Deborah tried hard to sound unconcerned.

The bed creaked alarmingly as Gil turned on his side to look at her. 'So as far as you're concerned I'm just another traveller on the road?' There was a strange undercurrent in his voice.

'Yes,' said Deborah, hoping that if she said it firmly enough she might even believe it. 'I know that you won't ... that we won't ...'

'What?' he said when she trailed off, wishing she'd kept her mouth shut.

Deborah glared at him through the darkness. 'You know what I mean!'

'You mean that I won't want to take advantage of the fact that I've got a girl conveniently tucked up in bed beside me?'

'Exactly. You've made it very clear that it's the last thing on your mind!' Deborah was uncomfortably aware of the note of pique in her voice, and added, 'And it's the last thing on mine as well!'

Gil propped himself up again to look down at her. The moonlight through the open window etched the soft lines of her face in silver. 'Is it?'

'Of course it is!' Deborah struggled to sound indignant. 'Just because Sylvie's infatuated with you doesn't make you irresistible to every woman.'

'What kind of man *do* you find irresistible, Deborah?'

'The kind that isn't like you!'

'That wasn't the impression I got when I kissed you,' Gil said unfairly. 'I wasn't expecting to find a passionate woman beneath that artless image you have.'

Deborah stared stubbornly up at the ceiling fan through the netting. Couldn't he hear the beating of her heart, boom, boom, boom like a deep, insistent drum? 'I don't know what you mean.'

'Don't you?' Gil moved with a speed that took her unawares, pinning her wrists to the bed as his body covered hers, and blocking her view of the fan. 'I'll show you.'

Deborah's eyes were huge as she stared into his face, racked with humiliating desire. Her senses, simmering since that first, devastating kiss, erupted into flaming life once more at the brush of his body. He was barely touching her, apart from the grip on her wrists, but her body tingled with his nearness and desire whispered over her skin. This was the man she had decided she hated; what then was this deep yearning, this trembling excitement at the prospect of feeling his lips on hers once more?

Her heart thudded with sickening, shaming anticipation as he lowered his head, and she closed her eyes so that he shouldn't read the naked desire in her face. Expecting a fierce, punishing kiss, she was unprepared for the soft, almost tender touch of his mouth, and her lashes flew open. Was he teasing her? She caught the glint of his eyes in the moonlight, as he lifted his head, and she was sure he had seen the flash of disappointment in her eyes, for his smile gleamed briefly before he found her mouth again.

This time, his lips were more insistent, and Deborah knew that he could feel her body's treacherous response. His hands left her wrists; she could easily push him away, but somehow her arms slid round his neck instead to pull him closer and deepen the kiss. Its fire was burning at the edge of control, desire beating insistently at the door. Gil's hands were hard against her skin, gathering her slender warmth tightly to him. His mouth plundered what was left of her resistance, warm and persuasive, promising ever greater delights, and Deborah abandoned thought of anything but the irresistible thrill of his kiss.

When his mouth left hers, she murmured in instinctive protest. Opening her eyes reluctantly, she saw that he was looking down into her face with an unreadable expression.

'Now you know,' he said softly, and her arms dropped from around his neck.

'You shouldn't have done that,' she whispered. 'Not just to make a point. I'm not Debbie.'

'No.' Gil rolled back to his side of the bed. 'No, you're not Debbie. Perhaps we'd both better remember that.'

Deborah lay quivering with unsatisfied desire long after Gil fell asleep. Her body ached with the need he had aroused in her, a need she had never felt before, but even while she wanted to hate him for playing with her she had to fight an overwhelming urge to slide over the bed and slip her arms around him. She wanted to press tantalising kisses along the back turned so firmly towards her, to wake him and turn him and make him love her properly.

Swallowing, she turned on her side and watched a tiny lizard scuttle across a bar of moonlight on the wall. Outside, the tropical night rasped with hidden insect life, unperturbed by the painful thumping of her heart. Deborah settled down to listen, convinced that she would never be able to sleep.

Gil was kissing her as if he loved her. His hands were tangled in her hair and he murmured endearments against her throat between hot, sweet kisses while she ran her hands urgently over his hard body...

'Wake up, Deborah!'

'No!' Deborah groaned, resenting being dragged out of her dream, but the strong hand on shoulder refused to let her go back to sleep. 'It can't possibly be time to get up yet,' she mumbled, rolling over and burying her head under the pillow.

Gil removed it firmly. 'It's more than time. You were dead to the world when I woke up, so I let you have a lie-in.'

'A lie-in?' Still groggy, Deborah groped for her watch on the bedside table and squinted at it in disbelief. 'It's only half-past seven. Lie-ins don't even start till nine o'clock!'

'They start at half-past six here,' said Gil unsympathetically, tying up the mosquito net. 'Now, hurry up.'

Deborah yawned and struggled to sit up, her hair a tousled cloud around her bare shoulders and her blue eyes sleepy. She blinked at Gil, who was looking crisp and cool in a short-sleeved khaki shirt and lightweight trousers, and tried to remember what she was doing in this unfamiliar room. And then the events of the day before came back in a sudden flood of vivid memories: losing her bag, sitting in the car next to Gil while the rain crashed around them, kissing Gil, wanting to turn and touch him...

Looking at him now, she found it impossible to believe that he had kissed her last night. He was as brisk as he had been the day before and Deborah, the wisps of her dream still lingering in her mind, began to think that it must all have been a dream after all. Her sarong had come loose during the night, and she clutched it around her protectively. Surely you didn't remember a dream quite that vividly?

Gil finished with the net and looked down at her. Catching his eye, Deborah was gripped by sudden, paralysing shyness. 'Did I snore?' she asked, just for something to say.

'No, but do you always smile when you're asleep?'

'Smile?' Deborah looked at him blankly.

'I've been watching you. You lay there sound asleep and smiling to yourself. It was almost unnerving!'

Deborah felt the colour creep up her throat as she imagined Gil watching her while she slept. 'I must have been dreaming.'

'What about?'

Her eyes slid away from his. 'I can't remember,' she lied.

There was a pause, and then Gil turned for the door. 'I'll go and get you some breakfast while you get dressed. Don't be too long. You're here to do a job.'

'I hadn't forgotten,' said Deborah with a touch of bitterness, but she decided in the shower that he was right. She had agreed to the job, for better or worse, so she might as well make the most of her stay here. She would enjoy being in Serok and not waste her time agonising about Gil.

He was waiting on the veranda when she emerged after her shower still plaiting her damp hair. There was coffee and papaya on the table and he was talking to a slight, elderly Indonesian woman dressed in the traditional sarong. 'This is Sarmi,' he introduced her, and Deborah smiled and shook hands. 'She normally cooks a meal and leaves it for me and since you're going to be in the office I've asked her to continue to cook for both of us.'

'Good,' said Deborah, and beamed at Sarmi in relief. Unusually for someone who enjoyed food so much, she was a hopeless cook and she was delighted to hear that she wouldn't have to face Gil's withering criticism of her efforts every night.

Her spirits restored, she ate a hearty breakfast and swung happily along beside Gil on their way down to the office. As she passed the frangipani tree, she reached up and plucked a flower to tuck into her hair. Gil looked irritable but said only, 'I suppose we'd better get you some more clothes at some stage. You can't wear that dress for three months.'

The office was a long, low building near the entrance to the camp. Deborah thought it looked very romantic with the palms rustling over the deep veranda, and when Gil introduced her to Deden, who acted as a local administrator, and Idja, the pretty typist, she decided that she might enjoy coming to work after all. She was less enchanted with the array of professional technology she found in the office that Gil had set aside for her.

'I don't have to use that, do I?' she whispered anxiously, viewing the word processor that sat on her desk with some alarm.

Gil looked annoyed. 'You told me you'd worked as a secretary!' he hissed, with an eye on the open door to the outer office.

'I have been a secretary. I've just always used a typewriter.'

'Well, you'll have to come out of the dark ages and learn to use a computer now,' he said unsympathetically. 'It's perfectly simple. Debbie can operate one in her sleep.'

'Bully for her,' muttered Deborah, but not quite loud enough for Gil to hear. She was getting sick of hearing how wonderful Debbie was.

'Deden and Idja are expecting you to be an experienced secretary who will know how to use all the equipment,' said Gil. 'I'm meeting Pascal at the dam site, so I suggest you spend the morning reading the instructions. I haven't got time to show you, but most of it is self-explanatory. I'll take you to the police station this afternoon to get you some papers, and tomorrow you can start some proper work. Deden and Idja have got plenty of their own work to do, so please don't distract them.'

He left her eyeing the computer, the telex machine and the photocopier uneasily, unable to decide which one of them looked the more intimidating, and her enthusiasm for the job rapidly waning. She had never expected to find such a well-equipped office in the middle of the jungle, and would have been much happier if the technology had been limited to a quill pen and carrier pigeons.

She made a half-hearted attempt to understand the instruction manuals, but soon admitted defeat. Ignoring Gil's order not to disturb Deden and Idja, she went through the office and cajoled Idja into showing her how the computer worked. Deborah had always had the ability to get on with people, and she and Idja were soon giggling together, with

Deden hanging indulgently over her shoulder to proffer his advice. Neither of them showed any surprise that Gil's supposedly efficient secretary-wife should be so transparently ignorant about modern office practice.

Prompted by Deborah, Deden and Idja told her about their families while endeavouring to explain the basics of word-processing, and they were laughing together when the door opened and Sylvie appeared. All three stopped laughing abruptly.

Sylvie raised an elegant eyebrow at the informal scene. 'You are obviously not very busy,' she said to Deborah, ignoring Deden and Idja. 'When I worked for Gil, I always had too much to do to waste my time chatting.'

Deborah eyed her with dislike. 'Did you want something?' Apart from Gil, she added mentally.

'I needed to see Gil,' Sylvie said in a haughty voice.

'Geel isn't here,' Deborah said, mimicking Sylvie's pronunciation of his name.

'Where is he?'

'Out,' said Deborah unhelpfully. 'I can give him a message if it's important.'

Sylvie's sulky mouth turned down. 'It's private.'

'I'm sure Gil wouldn't mind me knowing.' Deborah gave Sylvie a sweet smile. 'We don't have any secrets.'

'I shouldn't be too sure of that!' snapped Sylvie. 'Husbands and wives always have secrets from each other.' She walked with stiff, angry steps over to the window where she stood looking out, her back rigid with hostility. 'Shouldn't those two be doing some work?'

'If you're referring to Deden and Idja, they are working,' Deborah said coldly, but she didn't stop them as they glanced at each other and slipped quietly out of the room. 'As I am. So unless you want to leave a message for *my husband*——' she stressed the last two words '—perhaps you would leave and let us get on with what we were doing!'

Sylvie swung round, her black eyes blazing. 'You are so smug with talk about your husband, but you are not so lucky! Why do you think he never married you before? Because he never needed a secretary before, that's why! Why else would he marry someone like you with your shabby dress? A man like Gil needs a real woman, not a naïve girl. You are only here to do a job!'

Deborah got to her feet, glad that Sylvie would never know how right she was. 'Was there anything else?' she asked, knowing that her lack of reaction would irritate Sylvie more than anything.

'No, nothing else!' the older woman spat out. 'I was going to say to Gil that I would still help him with his confidential work since you will be so busy with typing the proposal, but now you can do all the work yourself!'

The outer door banged behind her, shaking the walls of the prefabricated building. Deborah blew the hair off her forehead and rolled her eyes at Idja, who shook her head.

'That woman makes trouble!'

The rest of the morning passed without incident, and Deborah even managed to get some sense out of the computer, although the telex machine and the photocopier still lurked as menacingly unknown quantities. She would just have to hope that Gil didn't want to use either of them that afternoon.

At half-past twelve, Deden went out to the *warung* by the gate of the camp and brought back chipped china plates full of spicy chicken soup. 'This is *soto ayam*,' he told Deborah. 'There is more to Indonesian cooking than *nasi goreng*! Tomorrow we will get you something different, and you can work your way through all our dishes.'

They ate companionably together in the office. Deborah got them to teach her some Indonesian words, and they were laughing uproariously when Gil reappeared. He stood in the doorway, and immediately the air tightened, as if he were charging it with his own electricity.

'Have you had some lunch?' Deborah waved her spoon at him, determined not to let him see how her reactions sharpened as soon as he appeared.

'Not yet.' Shutting the door behind him, he came into the room. 'I'm running a bit late.'

'Why don't you finish my soup?' she offered, struggling to sound normal.

After a momentary hesitation, Gil took the plate from her and leant on the edge of a desk while he ate. He said something in quick Indonesian to Deden, who laughed and replied with a glance at Deborah.

'What did he say?' Deborah asked Idja suspiciously.

'He asked Deden if you had behaved yourself. He said that sometimes you could be very bad!' They laughed at Deborah's affronted expression. Would he ever think of her as anything other than a naughty child?

'It's all right,' Deden added consolingly. 'I have told him that you are very nice and that it's easy to see why he is in love with you.'

Deborah's eyes met Gil's for a fleeting moment. Over the soup bowl, the light grey gaze held an ironic gleam that sent the blood rushing to her cheeks, and she looked quickly away.

'I'm ready to go whenever you are,' she said.

Gil held the door of the car open for her with what she was sure was mock courtesy. 'You seem to be getting on well with Idja and Deden.'

'I haven't been distracting them.' Deborah ruffled up at once. 'At least, not much,' she added with characteristic honesty. 'We're allowed to talk over lunch, surely? Or am I supposed to have taken a vow of silence?'

'It's a tempting thought,' Gil said drily. 'But I can't imagine you keeping it for very long. Anyway, I wasn't criticising. I know that neither Deden nor Idja wastes time in the office, and I wouldn't blame them if they'd found you distracting. I find you amazingly distracting myself!'

'I don't mean to be,' Deborah defended herself.

'I know. But you are anyway!'

She let Gil do the talking at the police station, grateful for his cool competence. He was on good terms with the senior officer, and, having explained the situation, got her a permit to stay until she had replaced her passport and arranged for a typed police report for insurance in what Deborah was sure was record time.

'You do have insurance, I suppose?' he said as they left the station with elaborate courtesies exchanged on both sides.

'Of course,' said Deborah with dignity. 'I even left the details with my father in case I lost my papers, which was just as well.'

'It sounds remarkably sensible for you,' Gil commented acidly.

'It was his idea,' she admitted. 'In fact, he insisted.'

'Poor man! I'm exhausted after looking after you for twenty-four hours. I pity him having had to worry about you for twenty-four years!'

'I know.' Deborah sighed. 'He's dying for me to get married so he can pass on the responsibility.'

Gil put out a hand to pull her back just as she was about to step into the path of a bicycle laden with enormous hands of bananas. 'I hope that anyone fool enough to marry you knows what he's taking on!'

He took her down to the market where they wandered up and down the narrow, muddy alleys between the stalls. Deborah's face was vivid with delight as she inspected rolls of batik, peered over a display of plastic trinkets made in Korea, tutted over the price of buckets and insisted on buying an armful of prickly red rambutans from an old man sitting patiently beside his woven baskets.

'We're supposed to be buying you something to wear,' Gil reminded her at last. The ants, disturbed from their exploration of the rambutans, ran up his arm, and he brushed them off with a resigned expression.

'I'll just get a couple of sarongs,' said Deborah. 'Prim said she would lend me anything else I needed.'

Gil looked down at her with a strange expression. 'You know, you're a very unusual girl. Most women would have been desperate at the prospect of having nothing to wear for three months.'

'Even Debbie?'

'Especially Debbie.' Gil fingered a bolt of material as they stopped by a stall. 'She always has to look perfect. She can't bear her nail polish to be chipped or to have a hair out of place. Sometimes I thought she spent far more time worrying about appearances than she did thinking about me.'

Deborah bent her head over the display of brightly coloured sarongs. 'She must be very attractive,' she muttered, not knowing what else to say. It was the first time she had heard Gil criticise Debbie.

'Yes.' He sounded oddly hesitant. 'She is attractive but she doesn't have a very warm personality. She has very definite ideas about how things should be done, and she can be critical if they don't match up to her standards. Of course, she's extremely efficient,' he added hurriedly, as if he had only just realised how unenthusiastic he sounded.

Deborah wished that she had never mentioned Debbie. Gil had been being nice, in an astringent sort of way, but his fiancée's name had introduced a new constraint, as if her efficient presence had come between them. Subdued, Deborah chose two sarongs with tops and then Gil bought her a simple cloth bag.

'This time, look after it!' he ordered gruffly.

'Oh, I will!' Deborah took it as if it were the latest Louis Vuitton.

A warning breeze ruffled the trees as they emerged from the market and Deborah drew a deep breath. She loved this moment, just before the downpour, when the light and the scents and the sounds of the tropics seemed to intensify.

'We'll never get back to the car in time,' said Gil, and the words were hardly out of his mouth before there was a deep rumble and the rain hit them. 'Come on!' Seizing Deborah's hand, he ran towards a *warung* whose position beneath the trees added to the meagre shelter afforded by its wicker roof.

Deborah held her packet of sarongs over her head as she was dragged after him, but she might as well not have bothered. They were both soaked before they reached the *warung*, and she laughed breathlessly as she dropped the parcel on to the bench and wiped the rain from her face with the backs of her hands. Her eyelashes were wet and spiky as she turned to Gil, her eyes alight with sheer pleasure in the moment.

Gil's shirt was dark and wet, and as she saw the way it stuck to the solid breadth of chest she realised how her own dress clung revealingly to her curves. Shaken by a sudden gust of physical awareness, Deborah sat down on the bench and concentrated on wringing out her dress.

'We may as well wait here till the worst is passed,' said Gil, sitting down beside her and ordering two glasses of coffee. They rested their elbows on the table and watched the rain swirling on the road. The wide avenue had emptied of pedestrians as if by magic; only one man with a wide conical hat trotted regardless of the rain, his loaded baskets balanced on a pole slung over his shoulder.

Deborah wanted to cling to the moment, to fix it in her memory. She felt as if she was tingling with awareness: the stall-holder pouring the water into the glasses, the smell of his clove cigarette pungent on the air; a yellow taxi cruising slowly past through the huge puddles, muddy waves rippling out from its wheels; the feel of the wet cotton against her skin; the hard wooden bench beneath her thighs. Most of all, she was aware of Gil. He sat still and self-contained beside her, his eyes following the taxi. His hair was slicked to his head and the dark hairs on his forearms were wet. Deborah could see the pulse beating in the shadow of his throat and the urge to lean over and press her lips to it was so strong that she almost flinched. The memory of his kiss pounded at her senses; she could taste his lips again, feel the hard touch of his body.

Gil turned his head, and she found that she couldn't look away. His eyes were cool and light, but they burned through her. Deborah forgot to breathe, and when the stall-holder placed the coffee in front of them she jumped. Her heart jerked and plunged and she cupped her hands around the glass to stop them shaking.

Gil pulled the paper the police had given him out of his pocket. 'You'd better keep this in case you get stopped,' he shouted above the noise of the rain.

'What does it say?' she asked. The paper was damp from the rain and she smoothed it out on to the table. The Indonesian was too complicated for her to understand.

'It says you belong with me.'

Deborah willed herself not to look at him. She gazed desperately down into her glass and as she felt her eyes crawl round towards his face made frantic efforts to fix them on the stain on the tablecloth, on the raindrops splashing through a hole in the roof, on the plastic crates advertising 'bir Bintang' stacked behind the table; but it was no good. Slowly, inexorably, her eyes were drawn to Gil's, until at last they stared at each other in a silence that jangled with tension, ignoring the sounds of the downpour.

'Just for three months, I hope.' Deborah's lips felt stiff and awkward.

'Yes.' The unnervingly light gaze shuttered and Gil looked away to pick up his glass. 'Just for three months,' he said.

CHAPTER SIX

GIL dropped Deborah back at the house. 'There's no point in your going back to the office this late in the day,' he said abruptly. 'I've still got some things to do. I'll meet you at the club later on.'

Left alone, Deborah sat on the veranda and twisted Gil's ring around her finger. The rain had stopped as suddenly as it had begun, and the palms dripped languorously in the steamy air. A brush-seller pushed his cart past with his mournful cry, '*Sa-pu*! *Sa-pu*!' She felt as if she was still reverberating from the look in Gil's eyes.

She *must* stop reacting like this. It's just a job, it's just a job, it's just a job, Deborah chanted to herself. If she was to get through the next three months, she had to learn to be as detached as he was. It might be unusual, but she had agreed to it like any other business arrangement. Gil was her employer, that was all. Somehow, it was easier to convince herself when Gil wasn't there with his disquieting eyes and his cool, unreadable expression.

Her dress was still damp, and she changed into one of the sarongs Gil had bought her before walking down to the club, swinging her swimming-costume from one finger. There was little more to the club than a bar, some tables under a bamboo roof and a greenish-looking pool, but it was evidently the social centre of the camp, and the first port of call for the engineers finishing work.

Prim was there, and she beckoned Deborah over, demanding to know how she had got on, on her first day at the office.

'It would have been a disaster if it hadn't been for Deden and Idja,' Deborah admitted, sitting down at the table and accepting a beer with a smile of thanks. 'Gil expects me to know everything about the office after one morning, and it took me all that time to learn how to turn the computer on!' It was a relief to be able to grouse to someone.

'He can be quite demanding, can't he?' Prim was sympathetic. 'I don't suppose it helps being his wife. He'll probably expect more of you than anyone else.'

'He'll be lucky,' said Deborah glumly.

'It's understandable, really.' Prim lowered her voice. 'He told me about his mother.'

Deborah wasn't sure how she was supposed to react to that. 'He did?' she said cautiously.

Fortunately Prim put her own interpretation on Deborah's hesitation. 'Oh, I know he doesn't talk about it, and I wouldn't dream of telling anyone else, but he did say one evening that he thought his mother had ruined his father's career. He was a civil engineer, too.'

Deborah tried to look as if she knew what Prim was talking about. 'Mmm,' she nodded.

'Gil said his mother was very frivolous and hated being stuck out in the middle of nowhere, and his father spent his whole time worrying about her. In the end, he gave up working abroad and settled for a job at home, but Gil said he was never quite the same. I got the impression that he adored his mother but found her utterly exasperating—but you must have met her, of course. What's she like?'

'She's wonderful,' said Deborah, who rather liked the idea of Gil having a frivolous mother.

'I thought she would be. I never quite believed Gil when he said that he was going to have a sensible wife who wouldn't cause him any trouble. He obviously thought that was what he wanted, but it's interesting that when it came down to it he fell in love with someone who wasn't sensible at all. I mean——' Prim broke off, worried in case she had caused offence, but Deborah merely sighed and grinned.

'You're quite right. I'm not very sensible. Gil certainly doesn't think I am.' She sipped thoughtfully at her beer. Had Gil's exasperating mother effectively pushed him into his arid-sounding relationship with Debbie? Had he deliberately chosen a girl who was everything his mother wasn't—practical, efficient, unemotional—so that he would be spared the scenes his father had endured? Deborah suspected that, in spite of everything, Gil would be too loyal to his mother to admit as much, particularly not to her. She was, after all, a perfect stranger, she reminded herself a little sadly, but at least it explained the lurking passion she sensed in him but which he had decided to deny when he'd asked Debbie to marry him.

'Ah, the new bride is having some time off!' Sylvie's mocking tones made her look up, her heart sinking as she saw the Frenchwoman sit down at the table. She was wearing a dramatically simple sheath dress in an icy blue colour, and looked as if she might have just stepped off a Paris catwalk.

Sylvie ran a disparaging eye over Deborah's brightly coloured batik outfit. 'I see you are adopting ethnic dress. Is that wise? Indonesian women are so delicate and elegant that they can wear those bright patterns, but you...' She trailed off with a pitying smile that was calculated to make Deborah feel huge and clumsy.

Deborah resisted the temptation to knock her beer all over Sylvie's pristine dress. 'I know,' she said sweetly, 'but don't say so in front of Gil, will you? He chose them for me.' It was worth the lie to see Sylvie's eyes snap at the reminder of who had first claim on Gil, and she pressed her advantage. 'He loves buying me presents, but I'm a simple girl at heart. Trivial things like clothes aren't very important to me. I tell Gil that now I've got him I don't need anything else!'

'Anyway, I think Deborah looks great,' said Prim, smothering a smile at Deborah's unconvincingly innocent expression. 'She's tall, but she's very slim, and she's got the kind of personality that can carry off anything.'

'Isn't that Michael?' Deborah asked, changing the subject quickly before Sylvie had a chance to reply. She nodded her head at Prim's husband who had just come out of the bar with a group of engineers.

'So it is!' Prim waved at him and they all came over to make a large, cheerful party round the table.

Michael kissed his wife and ruffled her curls as he sat down beside her. 'Gil's just getting the drinks... Ah, here is now.'

Deborah saw Gil as soon as he came through the door from the bar. He was carrying a tray of beers and hesitated for a moment as he looked for their group. Across the tables, their eyes met with jarring impact, and Deborah's heart turned over. The others around the table blurred into insignificance as she watched Gil make his way towards them. In contrast, he was in sharp focus, the lines of his body strong and distinct and the force of his personality catching at her breath.

'Gil!' Sylvie's husky voice broke the spell. 'We hardly had a chance to talk last night. Come and sit next to me!' She gestured charmingly to the empty seat beside her. 'As you see, your wife is surrounded by admirers!'

Deborah felt like pushing the poor young engineer by her side off his chair so that Gil would have to come and sit by her instead, but she had no choice but to put a brave face on it.

Gil set the tray on the table. His cool eyes flickered over the young men who sat on either side of Deborah. He didn't reply directly to Sylvie. Instead he put his hand on the top of Deborah's head and tilted her face back for a brief, possessive kiss.

'All right?' he asked her, for all the world an anxious husband who had been forced to leave his wife alone for an hour.

Deborah nodded as she struggled to control the rush of instinctive reaction to the touch of his lips. It might look as if he had a new husband's natural jealousy, stressing that she was his to the young men who sat on either side of her, but she knew better. He was acting a part, and the kiss had been directed at Sylvie. Her scalp tingled where he had laid his hand and she felt as if her mouth must be red and throbbing.

Gil had gone to sit next to Sylvie without fuss, and with an effort Deborah turned to Ian, who was sitting on her left, with a cheerful comment. Ian was tall and blond, with an easy warmth that Gil lacked. Why was it that Gil was so much more attractive? Deborah wondered, with one eye on his austere features. It wasn't as if he made any effort. All he did was sit there in that self-contained way of his, and her pulse went into overdrive. He obviously had exactly the same effect on Sylvie, who was leaning intimately close and talking in a low voice.

Deborah strained to hear, but as she was carrying on an amusing conversation with Ian at the same time she couldn't make out what they were talking about so intently. She did see Sylvie put an arm on Gil's shoulder and whisper in his ear, and nearly forgot to laugh at Ian's punch line.

'Come and have a swim, Ian,' she said, getting abruptly to her feet when, far from shaking Sylvie off, Gil smiled.

Ian got up with alacrity and followed Deborah as she marched off to the changing-rooms. If she had thought about it, Deborah would have known how the plain white swimming-costume flattered her slender curves and emphasised her long, slim legs, but she was too jealous of Sylvie to notice the admiring looks as she stalked to the pool and dived in.

The cool water refreshed her and after she had crawled up and down the pool a few times Deborah began to feel better. It was silly to let Sylvie upset her. She would have to beat her at her own game. Glancing at the pool, she saw that Gil was watching her larking around with Ian. He looked encouragingly grim, and, noticing that she had lost his attention, Sylvie pouted.

Satisfied, Deborah sat on the edge of the pool with Ian, talking and dangling her legs in the green water. She had deliberately sat looking away from the table, but she could feel Gil's eyes burning into her smooth brown back.

When she thought she had demonstrated that she couldn't care less if Gil spent his time talking to Sylvie, Deborah slung her towel around her neck and walked unhurriedly back to the table, wiping her face with the end of the towel as she went. Deliberately ignoring Gil, she was almost there when she risked a glance in his direction. He was staring at her as if he had never seen her before, and she was suddenly acutely conscious of her body in its skimpy covering. She faltered, feeling naked before Gil's light, intense stare, and in spite of the heat tiny goose-bumps rose on her flesh.

'Look at Gil!' Michael laughed. 'Anyone would think he'd never seen his wife's body before!'

Deborah didn't dare meet Gil's eyes. She glanced at Sylvie instead and was pleased to note that she was looking displeased at all the attention Deborah was getting. Encouraged, Deborah perched herself on the arm of Gil's chair and slid a casual arm around his shoulder. She might as well rub it in now that she had the chance.

'Gil knows all about me,' she said merrily. 'Don't you, darling?' Meeting Sylvie's dangerous glance coolly, she bent her head and kissed him quickly on the mouth before she had a chance to lose her nerve.

His body stiffened imperceptibly at her apparently careless kiss but his eyes when they finally met hers were deliberately expressionless. 'Not quite,' he said. He smoothed his hand down her spine, and Deborah felt herself quiver luxuriously like a cat. 'In fact,' he went on, 'the longer I know you, the more surprising I find you.'

'Women are a constant mystery,' Michael agreed, pulling Prim's hair affectionately, and she grinned at him.

Deborah envied them their easy affection. Prim and Michael's marriage was for real. They could be natural with each other, while she and Gil were merely playing a part. She forced herself to stay relaxed, but her body sang with awareness where it touched his. She could feel the hard muscles of his shoulder beneath her hand, and thought how nice it would be to rub the tension away and kiss the wary look from his eyes.

Suddenly, Sylvie stood up. 'I am going home,' she announced grandly.

'In that case, I'll have your chair.' It was a relief to move away from Gil and the fear that her hand might begin to move of its own accord. Deborah settled herself in Sylvie's seat and met the Frenchwoman's glare with a guileless look.

Having ceded her place, Sylvie had no choice but stalk off. Deborah watched her go, elated at her success. The atmosphere improved dramatically with the Frenchwoman's departure, and Deborah settled down to enjoy herself. She was on sparkling form and kept them all entertained until Gil got to his feet as abruptly as Sylvie had. 'You'd better go and get changed, Deborah. It's time we were going.'

There was a chorus of protest, but Gil was adamant, and Deborah trailed off reluctantly to put on her clothes. He was waiting for her as she came out of the changing-room, intent on not letting her get back to the table.

'What's the big hurry?' she grumbled, as he took her arm in an ungentle grasp and pulled her outside.

'I thought you'd done enough showing off for one night,' he said.

'I was having a good time,' said Deborah sulkily. She had to trot to keep up with his stride.

'So was Ian Matthews! Rather too good a time! You might have been a little less obvious.'

'What was there to be obvious about?'

His jaw worked convulsively, and his fingers dug into her arm. 'Ian's a good-looking young man, as he knows only too well. If you're thinking about asking him for help to get to Jakarta, you can forget it!'

'It never occurred to me,' she protested. 'I don't know what you're being so jealous about! I was just making conversation.'

'Is that what you were doing whispering together by the pool? I suppose all that splashing and giggling and fluttering your eyelashes was just making conversation too? We've got enough trouble with Sylvie forgetting she's married without you carrying on the tradition of faithless wives!'

'Oh, this is ridiculous!' Deborah was breathless as she stumbled after him along the rough road. It was dark now and the tropical night wrapped itself round them like a hot, sticky blanket.

'You're working for me, Deborah. You're here to play the role we agreed—and that doesn't include flirting with Ian Matthews! Don't forget who's paying you.'

'I can hardly forget with you reminding me every five minutes,' Deborah said waspishly. 'And I've been sticking to *my* part of the agreement. Everybody's convinced that I'm your wife.'

'Quite a little actress, aren't you?' he agreed with contempt. 'That was quite a performance you gave back there!'

'That's what you wanted, wasn't it? At least it got rid of Sylvie—no thanks to you!' Deborah was as angry as he was now. 'You might have got the part of a ridiculously jealous husband down to a fine art, but Sylvie's hardly going to be convinced by your performance as a lover!'

'What do you mean by that?' Gil demanded furiously.

'She could hardly avoid seeing the way you flinched when I kissed you.' Both flushed and angry, they had reached the house. 'It was like kissing an iceberg!'

Gil stopped so abruptly that Deborah cannoned into him. He swung her round so that her shoulder brushed against the frangipani tree, releasing a shower of fragrant white flowers. 'How did you want it to be, Deborah?' he said in a savage undertone. 'Like this?' Jerking her into his arms, he kissed her, a hard, thrilling kiss that caught Deborah unprepared. With no time to protest, she fell against him, her hands clutching instinctively at his chest for balance, and her lips opening beneath his.

He held her face between his hands, but as the kiss caught fire his angry grip became a caress. His thumbs drifted along her jaw and his fingers explored the soft, sensitive skin at the nape of her neck beneath the heavy plait. His mouth was demanding, but its insistence concealed an insidious delight that gradually vanquished the anger, leaving misunderstanding and uncertainty dissolved in a surge of intoxicating, unexpected passion.

Deborah was adrift, the night with its haunting fragrance of frangipani spinning round her. She was aware only of Gil's tantalising hands, of the compelling warmth of his lips, and she closed her eyes, abandoning herself to the gathering excitement that held both of them in thrall.

Gil's hands slid down her throat to her arms as if he might pull her closer, but at the last moment he changed his mind and lifted his head to look down into her dazed face.

'I can act as well as you, Deborah,' he said.

The spinning night steadied around her as reality hit her with the force of a slap. She could read the contempt in his face and lashed back without thinking.

'It's a pity you didn't do that before. Your technique isn't very impressive close up, but anyone watching might have been convinced—even Sylvie!'

Wrenching herself out of his grasp, she ran up the steps to the veranda and slammed the door shut behind her. She was shaking, and, terrified that she might burst into tears if she stopped to think, she went into the kitchen and began slamming pots around to reheat the meal Sarmi had prepared for them.

'You'll break something if you're not careful,' Gil said, appearing in the kitchen door. When

Deborah took no notice but crashed the wok on to the gas ring, he sighed. 'Don't you think you're over-reacting?'

'*I'm* over-reacting? What were you doing out there if not over-reacting?'

'I was making a point, that's all.'

'Fine! Now you've made it, we both know where we are. We can both pretend to be in love when required, but I have to try harder because I'm being paid for it!' Crash, bang went the pots. 'And since you're so keen on reminding me of my servile status I'd like my first week's pay now.'

'You don't need any money while you're here. You can put any drinks on the slate in the club and Sarmi will do any shopping you need.'

'I'd feel better with money in hand,' Deborah said, tossing the rice around the wok so aggressively that most of it fell out on to the cooker. 'Then I can see that I'm saving enough to get myself to Jakarta. That's why I'm here, after all.'

Gil prowled around the kitchen. 'You haven't earned a week's pay yet.'

'I think I have.' Deborah's angry blue eyes looked into ice-grey. 'After all,' she said deliberately, wanting to hurt him. 'I've kissed you four times now. I deserve some money for that.'

The ice in his eyes blazed. 'It's five times, if you're thinking of producing an invoice!' Turning on his heel, he went out, but reappeared almost immediately with a wad of notes. He dropped them contemptuously on to the bench beside her. 'There you are, Deborah. We don't want you to forget what you're here for, do we?'

The evening seemed interminable. They ate in a tense silence, neither willing to admit that they had no appetite. Afterwards Deborah pretended to read a book while Gil worked at his desk. She waited as long as she could and then went to bed, muttering an excuse. She wasn't really tired, but she couldn't bear the thought of climbing in next to Gil. At least this way she might have a chance of being asleep before he came.

For a while, she lay rigid beneath the netting, listening to a lone mosquito whine in ominous preparation for a dive, but she must have been more tired than she thought, for she had drifted off to sleep long before Gil left his papers. Vaguely aware of the bed sagging as he settled beneath the sheet, Deborah was too deep in dreams to protest at the hands that rolled her gently back to her side of the bed.

She woke once in the night. Her eyes opened languorously to find that her face was resting comfortably against Gil's shoulder. She lay on her side, and one of her hands clasped his forearm. She could smell his skin, feel its smooth texture beneath her cheek. It was rougher on his forearm, where her fingers tangled in the short dark hairs, and she rubbed her thumb over them in a sleepy caress.

She was curiously reluctant to move away. The rhythmic rise and fall of his chest as he slept was reassuring, and she was conscious of an over-whelming sense of security. In the serene place between sleep and wakefulness, Deborah wondered why she had been so angry with him, but it didn't seem to matter. All that mattered was that he was

there, and with a contented sigh she closed her eyes
and drifted back to sleep.

Over the next few weeks they fell into a routine
marked by an unspoken agreement to spend as little
time alone together as possible. The kiss and the
argument that had followed it were never referred
to, but the memory was always there, lurking,
waiting for an unthinking comment to explode in
vivid detail.

As Gil had warned, they were busy in the office,
and Deborah was glad that having so much to do
gave her less time to think about Gil. He was a
demanding boss, but she found that she enjoyed
the work, and although Gil was often exasperated
by her unorthodox methods she usually got the job
done in her own muddled way.

She liked working with Idja and Deden, too.
'Don't you women ever stop talking?' Gil said
grumpily, coming in one day to find Prim perched
on the edge of a desk and Deborah dispensing tea
and biscuits. 'There's always someone in here telling
you their life story!' he complained to Deborah later
in his office. 'The engineers are supposed to be out
on site, not hanging around the office. They can't
all have messages to go back to London!'

'Most of the time they just want someone to talk
to,' she explained. 'They come in to see if there's
any post, and stay for a chat.'

Gil flicked crossly through a draft report. 'You
never seem to have that much to say to me,' he
said. Deborah glanced at him, wondering if she had
imagined the note of jealousy in his voice, but his
expression was hidden behind the report.

'I think they find it easier to talk to a woman if they've got a problem,' she said carefully. Ian Matthews had poured his heart out to her only that morning. He had something of a reputation as a womaniser, and, having always rather taken his girlfriend for granted, he was now baffled and anxious about the fact that she seemed to have suddenly stopped writing. Deborah did little but listen sympathetically but Ian was pathetically grateful for her interest. 'They can get it off their chests rather than brooding about it.'

'And what terrible problem does Ian Matthews have that brings him in here day after day?' Gil asked nastily, but Ian was very much in awe of him and Deborah had no intention of discussing what he had told her in confidence. 'I'm always tripping over him,' Gil complained when Deborah gave a non-committal answer. 'At least when Sylvie was here we could work in peace!'

Sylvie herself missed no opportunity to exclaim at how disorganised Deborah's office was. She had changed tactics, and was bent on proving to Gil— in the subtlest possible way—what a mistake he had made in choosing Deborah. Deborah, she pointed out delicately, was hardly a professional secretary. She wore a sarong with frangipani or hibiscus in her hair, and although she began each day with a neat plait she clutched at her head so much as she struggled with the machinery that invariably by the end of the day it had all come undone. She was a little too familiar with the younger engineers, Sylvie suggested, and generally had no idea how to behave in a way that befitted a partner's wife.

As if to underline the point, she invited Gil and Deborah round to dinner. The food was delicious and Sylvie a gracious and elegant hostess. Deborah, who was tired after spending a frantic day typing an urgent report to be sent to London, knew that Gil could hardly fail to make the comparison. Debbie would have been able to compete with Sylvie, she thought dismally. If she was half as efficient as Gil was constantly claiming her to be, she would be able to knock out ten reports and still be able to produce a smart dinner party in the evening.

She glanced at Gil, expecting him to be admiring Sylvie's undoubted skills as a hostess, but he was looking down at his plate as he listened intently to something Pascal was saying. Unexpectedly, he looked across at her and smiled, a quick, reassuring smile, before turning back to Pascal so soon that Deborah wondered if it had merely been wishful thinking on her part.

The nights were the worst. During the day they could get by with a stilted politeness that only occasionally erupted into snappy arguments, but in the big bed there was nothing to keep the tension at bay. They lay without speaking on either side of the bed and listened to each other breathing.

Gil had never touched her again. Deborah told herself that she was glad, but sometimes, late at night, watching the ceiling fan circling slowly, she wished she had never made that gibe about wanting to be paid for kissing him. She ached with awareness of the lean body lying so close to hers and sometimes when she surfaced to feel his arm lying heavily across her, or his face buried in her hair, she would hug the feeling to her like a guilty secret.

If Gil ever woke to find her tangled against him, he never said. He was always up before her, and in the mornings when she awoke she was firmly on her side of the bed.

CHAPTER SEVEN

GIL came in from the site one afternoon to find Deborah staring ferociously at the computer. She didn't see him at first. Her tongue was sticking out to help her concentrate, and every now and then she would peer down at the manual beside her and mouth the instructions to herself.

'What *are* you doing?'

Startled out of her concentration, Deborah bit her tongue. 'Ouch!' She touched it gingerly with her finger. 'You gave me a fright.' She sent Gil an accusing look.

'I ought to be able to walk into my own office without my secretary passing out with shock,' Gil said, moving into the room. His eyes were alight with a strange mixture of amusement and exasperation. 'What's the problem?'

'I'm trying to work out the tabs so I can do the figures in columns. I don't know why they have to make everything so complicated,' she grumbled. 'It was much easier on an old typewriter. You just pressed the key where you wanted the tab to be. Now you have to have a degree in computer science to do the same thing!'

Normally Gil would have made some acidic comment about her inability to cope with straight-forward technology, but this time, although he shook his head in resignation, he was smiling reluctantly, and Deborah was so relieved that she smiled back.

'I'm afraid I'm not a very good secretary,' she apologised.

'You're doing all right,' Gil said gruffly. It was hardly an effusive compliment, but Deborah beamed.

'I am trying.'

'You're certainly that,' he said in a dry voice as if regretting being nice. He headed over towards his office. 'By the way, I've invited the local police chief and his wife round to dinner tomorrow night with Pascal and Sylvie.'

'Oh, dear,' said Deborah. 'Will I have to cook?'

'I think it might be appropriate if you made a bit of an effort. I've dealt with the police up to now, so I've got to know Tatang quite well, but Pascal will have to take over any problems on that front when I leave. I thought this would be a good opportunity for them to meet each other socially.'

When I leave. Deborah had almost forgotten that they would be going and that their pretence would come to an end. It was impossible to imagine leaving Terawati, saying goodbye to Gil, never seeing him again.

'I'm not a very good cook,' she warned him cautiously.

'You must be able to do something,' Gil said with a return to his irritable manner. 'It doesn't have to be up to Sylvie's standard.'

Just as well, Deborah thought, gazing morosely at the blinking light on the screen. 'I suppose Debbie can cook?'

'Yes.' He sounded hesitant as he straightened a pile of papers on her desk and then added in a burst of confidence, 'As a matter of fact, she's usually on a diet, and she never drinks, so she doesn't entertain very often.'

He looked as if he was remembering a series of very dull evenings, and Deborah sent him a speculative glance. She wondered if it was possible that he was realising that Debbie was not quite as perfect as he had remembered, and she allowed herself a brief glimmer of hope that he might be warming towards her.

It was a very brief glimmer, though. The next moment, Gil was back to his usual brisk self. 'You can take tomorrow afternoon off to give you time to get ready,' Gil said briskly. 'You might spend some time tidying up, too. I've never known anyone create so much mess. There are clothes all over the bedroom, and you never put the tops back on the shampoo or the toothpaste.' It had obviously been niggling at him for some time. 'It's not as if it takes any time. For someone who takes no interest at all in how they look, the bathroom looks as if a hurricane's been through it every morning!'

'If you didn't frogmarch me out of the house at the crack of dawn, I might have time to leave things tidy,' she retorted, disappointment sharpening her voice.

'You'd never get here in time unless I made you,' he snapped back. 'You *are* here to do a job.'

'More like slave labour,' Deborah muttered under her breath as he shut his office door behind him. 'If I'm going to have to cook and clean on top of everything else, I'll deserve a pay rise!'

Gil's comment about not trying to reach Sylvie's standard rankled and the next afternoon she took herself down to the market in a bicycle rickshaw, hoping for inspiration. Sylvie had managed to produce a meal that might have come straight out of a Paris restaurant. Deborah wandered up and down the stalls and decided that Sylvie must be a witch who had conjured the ingredients out of thin air. Perhaps she should be nicer to her, she thought gloomily, or she might find herself turned into a frog.

In the end she bought some rice, some doubtful-looking chicken and a lot of chillies to disguise the flavour. She quite enjoyed ransacking Sarmi's cupboards to find things to throw in the curry, although Gil winced at the mess when he came home.

'Is everything under control?'

'Of course,' said Deborah airily, turning up the flame under the wok.

Sylvie and Pascal arrived first. Sylvie looked typically sophisticated in a tight black dress and she raised an eyebrow at the reappearance of Deborah's blue cotton dress.

'You're so lucky, Deborah, not worrying about what you look like,' she said with a saccharine smile. 'I wish I could get away with wearing cheap clothes like you.' She glanced down at her own glamorous outfit with a satisfied smile.

'Deborah doesn't need to waste money on clothes which are as expensive as they are unnecessary.' Pascal gave his wife a look of reproof and came unexpectedly to the rescue. 'Her beauty comes from inside.' He smiled charmingly at Deborah. 'You would look just as lovely in a sack.'

'That's all this is, really,' said Deborah with a rueful glance at her shapeless dress, but she felt better for Pascal's support and hoped that Gil had heard him.

Tatang and his wife, Atiek, arrived shortly afterwards. Atiek was very shy and spoke little English, but as Deborah's Indonesian had improved dramatically after practising every day with Idja and Deden she was soon able to draw her into a conversation. She was just congratulating herself on the fact that it was all going very well when Gil sniffed.

'Is something burning, Deborah?'

Deborah fled to the kitchen. The chicken curry was a burnt, claggy mess and she nearly had a fit when she saw the rice. It was black with weevils.

'Gil!' she called, trying to sound casual.

'What is it?' he hissed, as he came into the kitchen.

'You remember I told you I wasn't a very good cook?' Deborah pointed at the stove.

Gil looked. 'Not very good was obviously something of an understatement!' He covered his eyes with his hand. 'Deborah's dish of the day—boiled weevils and carbonised chicken bones.'

Deborah couldn't repress a giggle. 'You'll have to keep them talking,' she said, picking up a plate. 'I've got an idea. I'll be back in a minute.'

Slipping out the kitchen door, she ran down the street until she found the old man squatting by his *sate* cart. A paraffin lamp spluttered as he cooked her an enormous pile of delicious chicken *sate* with

a spicy peanut sauce. Watching the unhurried grace
of his movements, Deborah wished that she could
be that dignified.

When the plate was full, she ran back to the house
and burst into the living-room. Her hair swung over
her shoulders and her blue eyes sparkled.

'Supper is served!' she cried gaily, setting the
plate of *sate* on the table with panache. 'I made
such a mess of the cooking that I've got you something nice to eat instead!'

Sylvie looked pleased at the thought of Deborah's
supper being a disaster, but she was less happy when
she saw how the others were enjoying themselves.
Pascal and Tatang applied themselves to the *sate*
with enthusiasm and even Atiek became animated
at Deborah's frank admission of failure.

Deborah breathed a sigh of relief and caught Gil's
eye across the table. He rolled his eyes and tried to
look disapproving, but a smile crinkled the edges
of his eyes. Sylvie noticed too, and picked up a stick
of *sate* fastidiously.

'Not everyone can cook,' she said to Deborah
patronisingly. 'I am sure you have other talents.'

Deborah tried to think of one, and failed. 'Not
really,' she said with disarming honesty.

'That's not true,' protested Pascal. 'You are very
good with people. Look how much all the engineers like you! I know that Gil would certainly not
agree that you have no talents.' He turned to Gil
for support, but Gil was looking at Deborah.

'Deborah is talented at life,' he said.

Pascal wagged his knife at Gil in admonishment.
'I hope you realise what a lucky man you are, Gil!'

Deborah was blushing in embarrassment, but when she risked a glance at Gil the smile was still lurking and his eyes were so warm that her heart jolted, and she put down her *sate* stick uncertainly.

'I'm beginning to,' he said.

After the traumas of entertaining, Deborah was glad that she had a weekend away to look forward to. Prim had suggested that they should drive down to the coast and forget about hydro-electricity for a couple of days. 'Those men could do with a break, and so could you,' she said to Deborah. 'It takes about four hours to get to the beach, and we stay the night in little wicker huts. You'll love it.'

Deborah did love it. Her spirits soared as they drove down through the hills. She loved the dripping green jungle, she loved the banana trees lining the lower roads, she loved the mangrove swamps. The roads, never very good, steadily deteriorated until they were little more than red mud, and the convoy had to keep stopping to push each other out.

'Isn't this fun?' said Deborah when it was their turn to bog down. She was enjoying every minute. Always the first to jump out and help, she was covered in mud, but her eyes shone bright and blue.

Gil looked at her and shook his head at her enthusiasm. 'Great fun,' he said drily as he went to push behind.

They passed isolated villages where the children ran after them shouting in astonishment, and a series of increasingly precarious bridges. Gil made Deborah get out as he drove across the rickety planks, and she danced behind him, unperturbed by the gaps or the wobble of the bridge beneath her.

'Are you always this easy to entertain?' he asked as she climbed in beside him again, breathless and laughing. 'If I'd known that all you wanted was to be rolled around in some mud and sent out to dice with death on rotten planks, I'd have laid on something long ago!'

Deborah grinned. 'I don't mind where I am,' she said, settling into her seat. 'But I do love trips like this!'

Gil put the car into gear and let out the clutch. 'Debbie would hate it,' he said.

Sometimes Deborah completely forgot about Debbie's existence, and her name was always like a glass of cold water in her face. Gil couldn't fail to see how hopelessly unsophisticated she was compared to his fiancée. She made a show of studying the map, not that it marked any of these 'roads'.

'She's obviously got more sophisticated tastes than I.'

'I don't think it's a question of sophistication,' said Gil, glancing at her. 'Debbie doesn't have your capacity to enjoy herself. She doesn't get very excited about anything,' he said slowly, as if realising it for the first time. 'You seem to be happy wherever you are.'

Deborah wondered how happy she would be without him. The map danced in front of her eyes and she put it back on the dashboard. 'I expect I'm just undiscriminating,' she said with determined brightness.

Even Gil admitted that the beach was worth the arduous trip. Deborah was ecstatic when she saw

it. Coconut palms leant elegantly over the burn-
ingly white sand at impossible angles, their fringed
leaves rustling almost imperceptibly in the gentle
breeze, and the sea was a limpid turquoise, deepen-
ing to a dark, intense blue beyond the reef.

A row of simple wicker huts stood back from the
beach and in the clearing beyond was the small restaurant that in Indonesia was inevitably found in
the middle of nowhere.

Deborah stretched out her arms and turned her
face up to the sun. 'It's perfect!'

'You might think it's less perfect when you see
the bed we have to share,' said Gil, coming up
behind her. 'I've been talking to Prim. There's a
bed missing from one of the huts, and the unani-
mous opinion seems to be that we should share the
single bed that's left.' His voice was dry. 'None of
the single men wants to share—understandably—
with one of their hulking great colleagues, Michael
claims to have a bad back, and Sylvie is so shattered by the trip down that she says she can't
possibly consider it.'

'There's hardly room for one person, let alone
two,' said Deborah when she saw the narrow bed.
The image of sleeping in it pressed up to Gil's lean
body was too vivid for comfort. 'We'd be better
off sleeping on the floor.'

'I don't advise it,' said Gil, nodding at the gap
at the bottom of the wicker walls. 'There are snakes
round here, not to mention all the other creepy-
crawlies. You might end up with a bedfellow you
like even less than me.'

Surprised at the oddly bitter note in his voice,
Deborah glanced at him, but his expression was as

unreadable as ever. Was he thinking about the night too, about how they would have to lie close together? It was bad enough trying to avoid touching each other in the big double bed. How were they going to cope tonight?

She turned away to hide her expression and pulled the wedding-ring off her finger.

'What are you doing?' Gil asked sharply.

'It's so loose, I thought I'd take it off before I lost it,' she said, putting it away carefully in the pocket of their bag. 'I should really get it tightened.'

'I hardly think it's worth it,' he commented in a hard voice. 'We haven't got that much longer.'

His words echoed in her ears as Deborah washed the mud away in the sea and then sat in the shade combing out her hair and drinking the milk from a fresh young coconut. Gil sat beside her, resting his arms on his knees and narrowing his eyes at the glare of the white sand. His body was brown and hard, smoothly muscled, and Deborah's fingers itched to reach out and touch him. The urge became so strong that she got up with a stifled gasp and ran to the sea. The water was cool and refreshing after the sand which had burnt her bare feet.

She floated on her face, opening her eyes beneath the water. It was so clear that she could see the brilliant colours of the tiny fish darting beneath her, their speckled shadows reflecting on the clean white sand below. Why couldn't she stop thinking about Gil's bare back and how it would feel beneath her fingers? Why was she wasting precious minutes in this beautiful place imagining the night to come, when she would have to lie close beside him in that narrow bed?

Turning on her back, Deborah stared at the sky, but the glaring, empty blue offered no distractions from the disquieting images that simmered in her mind. They made her stupidly shy of Gil when she walked back up the beach, and she dropped down as far away from him as possible, resenting this uncomfortable awareness for spoiling her day. She had been so happy on the trip down, she had been happy when she saw the beach, she had been happy until she'd seen that narrow bed. Now all she could think about was the night and Gil's hard body. She was desperately afraid that her own body might betray her into... what?

A beetle scurried past her foot and ploughed busily up the mound of sand she had pushed up with her toes. Deborah watched it with a blind intensity as the truth hit her with a sickening sense of despair.

She was afraid that her body would betray her into revealing how much she loved him.

It was so obvious that she wondered why it had taken her so long to realise. Of course she was in love with Gil.

I hardly think it's worth it, he had said, reminding her that their pretence would soon be at an end. It wasn't worth falling in love with him, either, although in her heart Deborah knew it was too late. She didn't dare look at him in case the knowledge was branded across her face. He was finding it difficult enough coping with her for three months, without the added embarrassment of her falling in love. She winced when she remembered how he had disliked Sylvie's attentions; she didn't want him to think of her like that. His opinion of her was low enough as it was. He was probably counting the days until he could pay her off and shut her out of his life with a sigh of relief.

Her eyes followed the beetle's progress as it clambered over every obstacle in its way. Why didn't it go round? she wondered dully.

How was she going to get through the next month without Gil guessing how she felt? He would be appalled, embarrassed. It wasn't as if he hadn't made his feelings for her perfectly clear. Theirs was a business relationship, that was all. He had loved Debbie, neat, sensible, efficient Debbie who could type and cook and always put the top back on the toothpaste; what chance was there that he would ever fall in love with her, the complete opposite? He would shudder at the very thought!

'You're very quiet, Deborah,' Pascal commented, and across him she saw Gil look up quickly. 'Is everything all right?'

'Of course,' she said, too loudly. Of course she was all right. She was bouncy, breezy Deborah, happy wherever she was. She would get over Gil; of course she would.

She spent the rest of the day being determinedly cheerful. She swam and splashed and ran after frisbees and distributed food and drink, all with a fixed, brittle grin. By the time the sun set in a spectacular display of red and gold, her face felt as if it would crack with the effort of smiling, and she was grateful for the gathering darkness that hid her expression.

They had a cheerful meal at the little restaurant by the light of a hissing paraffin lamp, and sat on when they had finished, talking and laughing together. Deborah managed to get through the meal without looking at Gil once.

'It's a beautiful night,' said Sylvie, who had recovered from the rigours of the journey to look as immaculate as always. She glanced at Deborah and then leant towards Gil. 'Last time we sat on the beach in the moonlight and talked for hours. Do you remember, Gil?' Her voice was low and husky, but Deborah heard every word.

'How could I forget?' said Gil, expressionless. 'In fact, I think it's time I showed my wife just how lovely the moonlight can be.' He stood up and came round to Deborah, smoothing his hand down her hair in a caress that made her shiver. 'Come for a walk, Deborah.'

There were grins and knowing looks at Gil's impatience to get his new wife alone in the moonlight, but Sylvie's face was dark with chagrin.

'That woman's a menace,' Gil said, as they walked down to the sea.

'Did you really talk for hours in the moonlight?' Deborah asked, unable to keep the note of jealousy from her voice.

'It felt like it. I thought I'd escaped from her for a while, but she tracked me down, and then I had to sit there while she talked at me about how Pascal didn't understand her and how difficult it was being a cultured woman trapped in the cultural desert of an engineering camp.'

'Why doesn't she go back to France if she feels like that?'

'I tried suggesting that, but she was unstoppable in full flow.' He glanced down at Deborah's averted face, shadowed by moonlight. 'I'm glad you're here. It would be even harder to avoid her if I didn't have you as an excuse.'

An excuse. That was all she was. Deborah stared out at the long strip of moonlight shimmering on the water. The sea barely rippled against their bare feet.

'We may as well go for a walk since we're here,' said Gil, after a moment, and they turned in silence and began to walk along the water's edge, side by side but not touching. Deborah's mouth was dry with the longing to reach out for him, to throw her arms around him and tell him that she loved him. It's not worth it, she reminded herself.

At the end of the bay, they sat on the soft sand, both reluctant to rejoin the party. It was quiet in the darkness. The sea whispered against the sand, and occasionally there was a dull thud as a coconut relinquished its hold and dropped to the ground. In the distance, they could hear faint shouts of laughter from the restaurant.

'They're probably imagining us exchanging passionate kisses in the moonlight,' said Gil.

Deborah could imagine it too, so vividly that she ached. She remembered how he had kissed her before, and how her body burned at the merest brush of his fingers. Her pulse thudded at the memory. All he had to do now was to turn to her, pull her down on to the soft sand, and kiss her the way he had kissed her under the frangipani tree. She would wrap her arms about his neck and he could run his hands over her eager warmth and together they could succumb to the desire flaming between them.

All he had to do was turn.

But Gil didn't turn. He lay back on the sand without her and looked up at the night sky. It was dense with the bright, massy stars of the southern hemisphere.

'There's the Southern Cross,' he said, pointing. 'And there's the Plough.' His voice sounded as cool as ever and Deborah knew that the thought of kissing her had never crossed his mind.

She tried to pull herself together. If he could sound that normal, so could she. 'I always think it should be called the Saucepan,' she croaked, and hurriedly cleared her throat.

Gil smiled. 'That sounds very prosaic coming from a romantic like you.'

'I'm not that romantic,' she protested.

'Yes, you are. You don't take life very seriously, do you? You just float along having fun and assuming there'll always be a happy ending.'

Deborah curled her toes into the sand. She *had* been like that, but not any more. This was one time when she couldn't envisage a happy ending.

'You're like my mother,' Gil went on. 'It never occurs to her to worry about mundane things like paying bills or what time it is or how she's going to get from A to B. She assumes that someone will always be there to sort things out for her, and of course there usually is.'

'What's she like?' Deborah asked curiously.

'She's impossible,' said Gil with a sort of resigned affection. 'She's irresponsible and frivolous, but so charming she always gets off with it, which is even more infuriating. My father wore himself out trying to cope with her. He could have had a wonderful career, but she was hopeless at being an engineer's wife. I always vowed that when I got married my wife would be as different from Mother as possible. She can be emotionally draining, either on cloud nine or in the depths of despair. You never know what she's doing. She's always launching into madcap schemes, and gaily drifting on to something else when she gets bored, leaving someone—usually me—to clear up the mess she leaves behind her.'

Gil shook his head with a reluctant smile at the thought of his exasperating mother. 'It's impossible to stay cross with her, though. She's always so pleased to see you, and so grateful for sorting her out. My father died when I was still at school, and I had to take over all her affairs. She's simply incapable of understanding her finances. I've tried to explain to her about money, but it just goes in one ear and out the other. She just says, "Of course, darling," and carries on ignoring bills. I don't suppose she's ever looked at a bank statement in her life!'

'She sounds a bit of a responsibility,' said Deborah, who rarely looked at her bank statements either. She thought Gil's mother sounded fun, but she could imagine how such an extravagant personality had forced him to become more and more sensible as he dealt with the problems she caused. If his mother had been as homely and sensible as Deborah's, he might have had a chance to rebel himself. As it was, he had had to be prudent and reliable from such an early age that it had become a matter of habit.

'She is a responsibility,' Gil agreed. 'And not just a financial one. I never know where she is or what she's up to. That's why I decided long ago that my wife had to be a support, not another responsibility. I wanted someone practical enough to cope with living overseas, someone discreet and responsible who would be able to work with me to build up the firm.'

'Like Debbie?' Deborah forced herself to ask.

He hesitated. 'Yes,' he said at last, but he didn't sound very sure. 'I've worked hard to get this far. I can't afford to end up with the wrong wife,' he went on, as if trying to convince himself. 'I've seen what can happen with my father, and now with Pascal. His mind's not on the job at the moment because of Sylvie. It's not just my future that depends on the success of the firm. Pascal's does too, of course, but also all the people who work for us. Debbie's about as different from my mother as she could be. That was one of the reasons I asked her to marry me. My mother had been being particularly scatty, and I'd had enough of worrying. Debbie was cool and calm and unemotional. I knew that I would never have to worry about *her*.'

Deborah let the sand trickle through her fingers. He could hardly make it clearer: she was the last type of girl he would consider marrying. He might not be in love with Debbie, but she was the kind of wife he wanted. Perhaps he was right. Perhaps he would be better off with a girl like Debbie who wouldn't distract him or irritate him.

She tried to imagine what her own future would be. She had never given it much thought before. She had wanted to travel, to have a good time, that was all. It wasn't much of an ambition, but now she had lost even that. She had been looking forward to Australia, but now the prospect of being there alone filled her with despair. All she wanted was to be with Gil, and there was no place for her in his future.

'I think I'll go back,' she said, getting to her feet. 'I'm tired.'

In silence, they walked back along the beach to the wicker hut. Deborah was too miserable to even worry about the single bed. She washed the salt from her skin and wrapped a clean sarong around her, and slipped in beside Gil. He lifted an arm so that she could settle against him and then folded it across her bare shoulders. Its warm, solid strength was inexpressibly comforting, and in spite of herself Deborah found herself relaxing. Her cheek rested against his chest and she could hear the steady beat of his heart. The moonlight through the wicker wall chequered their bodies as if they were one.

She stirred and settled herself more comfortably, slipping an arm naturally across his body, and his other arm came round to enclose her.

'It'll be all right.' Gil's voice came softly from above her head and Deborah nodded. He would never love her, but at least for tonight she could lie in his arms. For tonight that would be enough.

CHAPTER EIGHT

WHEN Deborah opened her eyes the next morning, she was still wrapped in Gil's arms.

'Don't tell me you're awake at last!' His voice was low and warm with amusement. 'I don't need to ask how you slept!'

Deborah stirred reluctantly. 'You should have woken me.'

'I didn't like to disturb you. You were sleeping so comfortably with that serene smile you have when you're dreaming.'

His throat was tantalising close. Still half asleep, Deborah watched his pulse beating and wondered how he would react if she pressed her lips to it. She strummed with the need to kiss him, and all at once it seemed absurd not to tell him. What better time could there be than now, when there was nothing between them but inhibition?

'Gil?' she whispered in a strangled voice and her fingers tightened against his chest, but before she could go any further there was a bang on the door.

'Are you two lovebirds planning to sleep all day?' shouted a cheerful voice. 'If you don't hurry up you'll miss breakfast.'

It was enough to jerk Deborah out of her sleepy trance. She sat bolt upright, horrified at how near she had come to confessing to Gil. A moment later and she would have had to watch the distaste spread across his face as he realised what she meant.

'We're just coming,' she called, and stood up, clutching her sarong to her chest, desperate to get away from the dangerous closeness of Gil's body.

'What's the rush?' said Gil, watching her. 'We're supposed to be on holiday.' He paused. 'What were you going to say before we were so rudely interrupted?'

'Oh, nothing, nothing important. I can't remember now.' Deborah found that she was gabbling as she turned her back on him and retied her sarong. 'I don't want to miss breakfast. I'm starving. See you there.'

She practically ran out of the hut, and spent the rest of the day avoiding being alone with him. Ian was in a sombre mood, having still not heard anything from his girlfriend, and Deborah sympathised so much with his valiant attempts to appear cheerful that she devoted herself to cheering him up. After hearing that he had had an uncomfortable trip down to the beach, squeezed into a jeep with three others, she offered him a lift back in Gil's car. It would be more comfortable for him, as well as for the others in the jeep, and she seized on the chance to have someone else in the car during that long drive back to Terawati.

Gil, when approached in front of everyone else, had no choice but to second Deborah's invitation, but his face was set in grim lines as they bumped back along the mud tracks. Deborah thought miserably of how different she had felt as they had driven towards the beach, but she forced herself to chatter feverishly until Ian and Gil's lack of response drove her to seek refuge in brooding silence too.

'Was it really necessary to give him a lift?' Gil asked through clenched teeth when they had dropped Ian off at last.

'I just thought it would be more comfortable for him.'

'He can't have felt very comfortable with you fawning over him all day,' he said savagely. 'I thought Sylvie was bad enough!'

Deborah was too tired to explain about Ian. Let Gil think she was attracted to the younger man. He would have less chance of recognising the truth that way.

'At least he's good company, which is more than you were. You had a face like concrete all day.'

'Was I supposed to enjoy the spectacle of my wife making an exhibition of herself with another man?'

'I'm not your wife,' she pointed out, in a tight, hard voice.

'I'm paying you to behave like my wife,' said Gil after a frozen pause. 'I'd like to get my money's worth.'

'That's all you care about, isn't it?' she cried. 'No wonder Debbie didn't want to marry you!'

Gil refused to answer that, and they barely exchanged a word for the rest of the evening. The atmosphere was still glacial the next morning and Deborah was glad that Gil was going to be up at the dam for most of the day. It meant that she could pretend that all was as normal, even though she felt a tight fist of misery inside. Gil despised her. She was just a commodity he had bought and would discard when he no longer had any use for her.

When the weekly mail bag arrived, she seized on the chance for distraction and began sorting the letters into the pigeon-holes. She had one from her mother, and seeing that familiar handwriting she felt an unaccustomed wave of homesickness. She put it aside to read later, and carried on with the sorting.

Gil had a number of letters, mostly official-looking ones, but there was also an aerogramme addressed in round feminine lettering that looked as if had been written along a ruler. Deborah's eyes narrowed, and she turned the letter over to see who it was from. Sender: Miss Debra Clark.

Of course, Debbie *would* spell her name like that! She probably signed the letter 'Debi', with a heart over the 'i' too, Deborah thought savagely.

She itched to know what was in the letter. It was the first time Debbie had written to Gil since she had refused to marry him at such short notice.

Putting the aerogramme on top of Gil's pile of letters, she waited for him to comment when he came in, but he was still in a foul mood and merely picked them up and went into his office, shutting the door firmly behind him.

Frustrated, Deborah vowed that she wouldn't give him the satisfaction of knowing that she cared, but by the time they were sharing another awkwardly silent meal that night she could bear it no longer.

'What did she want?' she burst out.

'What did who want?'

'Debbie,' she said, tight-lipped. 'She hasn't written to you before. Why should she suddenly send you a letter now?'

'I fail to see that it's any of your business,' said Gil in a glacial voice. 'But, if you must know, she wrote to say that she still considers our engagement to be on. She suggested we get married when I get back to London. She's due some leave about then.'

'How convenient for her!' Deborah pushed her rice angrily around her plate. 'It suits her to get married now, so she expects you to fit in with her arrangements. I hope you're not going to take her up on it?'

'Of course I'll think about it,' snapped Gil. 'Debbie would be an ideal wife for me.'

'What's ideal about someone who couldn't be bothered to change her plans to marry you when you wanted?'

'I suppose you think you'd be a better choice?' he said unpleasantly.

Yes, she wanted to cry. Yes, I would be a better wife. I'd love you and care for you and kiss the tired lines from your face at the end of the day.

Instead, she pushed back her chair and stood up. She began clearing up the table with much clattering and banging of dishes. 'Well, if you want to lumber yourself with someone boring and sensible and so stupid she can't even spell Deborah properly, go ahead!'

'I don't need your permission.' A nerve beat furiously in Gil's cheek. 'As you pointed out so clearly last night, you're not my wife.'

'I'm not losing any sleep over it!' Deborah flung at him over her shoulder as she headed for the kitchen. 'Believe me, I'm counting the days until this particular job is over!'

How was it possible to argue so bitterly with someone you loved so much? she wondered desolately in bed that night. She had always had the sunniest of natures, but the slightest comment from Gil had her snapping like a virago. He would be glad to get rid of her.

The hostility was still rigid between them when Gil walked into her office a couple of days later. He was holding one of the telexes that had arrived that morning. 'I've been called to Jakarta to meet the Minister. He's considered our proposal for the second stage of the scheme and he's going to let me have his decision tomorrow.'

'I'm sure he'll give you the contract,' said Deborah impulsively, forgetting her antagonism as she saw the worry in his eyes. She knew how important the contract was for the firm.

'I hope you're right.' Gil dropped the telex on her desk. 'You'd better book two seats on the flight tomorrow morning.'

'Is Pascal going with you?'

'No, you are. I'll have to take the government liaison officer and his wife out to dinner, so you can come and help me entertain them. We may as well get you a new passport at the same time.'

They had to leave very early the next morning to get to Parang in time for the flight. Deborah was thoughtful as they drove down the same road she and Gil had first travelled together. She was a different person from the light-hearted girl who had fallen in front of Gil's car. How different would her life have been if she had kept her bag on her lap that day? She felt cold at the thought of never having met him, never having loved him. Even if she never saw him again at least she would have known him, and a new determination seized her to make the most of the little time they had left together. It was silly to waste it arguing.

The plane to Jakarta was waiting on the runway at Parang when they arrived. Deborah eyed it nervously. She hated flying at the best of times, and this was an old-fashioned plane with propellers. It would never get off the ground.

Her conviction grew as she stared out through the small window at the blurring propellers, and she linked her hands in her lap to stop them shaking. As the plane lumbered to the end of the runway in preparation for take-off, her grip tightened until the knuckles showed white and she fixed her gaze on the seat-back in front of her.

Suddenly, Gil reached over and covered both her hands with one of his. 'Why didn't you say you were scared of flying?'

'I always feel so silly,' said Deborah, clinging gratefully to his hand. Its warmth and strength were wonderfully comforting. 'I don't mind it once the plane's up, but I hate take-off.'

'It must be a bit of a drawback for someone who wants to travel as much as you do,' Gil commented with a hint of amusement.

'Why do you think I came overland?'

He held her hand until the stewardess came round with a box of refreshments each. The worst of her fear had passed, but Deborah was reluctant to let go of his fingers, and she was guiltily relieved when Gil, having decided against the luridly coloured confection, sticky rice cake and carton of cold tea, pushed his box aside. He pulled out a report to read, but after a glance at her face he sighed and clasped her hand once more, and continued to read one-handed.

Jakarta was as intriguing as Deborah remembered. Modern skyscrapers loomed over the low, red-roofed houses of the kampongs; peaceful tree-lined avenues and narrow *gangs* barely wide enough for two people to pass led into wide highways jammed with impatiently hooting traffic; women selling *sate* piled on banana leaves squatted outside gleaming shopping centres—all shrouded in the damp heat and shimmering petrol fumes and vibrant with the sound of blaring taxi horns, traditional street calls and the crackle of loudspeakers from the mosques, calling the faithful to prayer.

Their hotel was near the centre, but so cool and quiet that it might have been in a different city altogether. Deborah had never stayed in such an expensive hotel before, and she felt horribly conspicuous in Prim's dress, which was completely the wrong shape for her. Gil had refused to let her wear her blue dress. 'It's too shabby,' he had said firmly. 'I'm not taking you dressed like Orphan Annie. Besides, it's unsuitable. Jakarta's a Muslim city. You'll have to borrow something with sleeves.'

Now she felt like whispering as Gil checked in. 'I'm going off to this meeting after lunch,' he said as they waited for the lift to their room. 'I suggest you go to the British Embassy to apply for a new passport, and then go and buy yourself some decent clothes. Mrs Seraputri is very smart,' he warned her, giving her some money. 'See if you can make a bit of an effort for a change. Oh, and perhaps you'd post this for me?' He pulled an airmail letter out of his briefcase and handed it to her.

It was a letter to Debbie. Deborah stared down at the name, unsure of whether she longed to know what he had said or dreaded it.

'I've told her that I think it's better to forget the whole question of an engagement for the time being,' Gil said, very casually. 'As far as I'm concerned, she made her decision when she refused to get married, and it seems strange for her to suddenly change her mind.' He paused, glancing at Deborah. 'We both need to think about what we really want,' he finished.

What *did* Gil want? Deborah wondered when he had gone off to his meeting. Her heart beat a little faster, hoping against hope that he might learn to love her instead, but her head told her not to be foolish. He had given her no indication that he felt any of the desperate desire that consumed her. He was as brisk as ever, with that edge of exasperation whenever he looked at her, as if she reminded him all too closely of his mother. He had been so determined not to saddle himself with another irresponsible woman. Even if he *had* decided that he didn't want to marry Debbie after all, it didn't mean he would turn round and fall for someone who was the complete opposite. There was absolutely no reason for her heart to start singing as she dropped Gil's letter to Debbie in the postbox. She mustn't make a fool of herself.

But in spite of her stern warnings to herself Deborah spent the afternoon wondering about Gil, wondering what he had felt when he'd written to Debbie, wondering what it would be like if he kissed her again. He was free! Her nerves fluttered at the thought of the evening to come. She was determined not to let Gil down. If she was smart and well behaved, perhaps, just perhaps, he might start to love her...

She wanted to find a dress that would dazzle him with her sophistication, but her confidence grew less and less as she wriggled in and out of the outfits on display in the expensive shopping plazas. She looked awful in everything, she decided, gloomily waving down a taxi to try somewhere else.

The taxi driver, having discovered where she lived, whether she was married and what she was doing in Jakarta, was just asking her why she had no children, when Deborah was struck by inspiration. Leaning forward, she asked him to take her to a tailor in the Chinese district.

Four hours later, she was back at the hotel, feeling a queer mixture of excitement and trepidation. She had found a beautiful wild silk in jade-green, and while the tailor had made it up into a simple cheongsam-style dress she had had time to find some shoes, some make-up and a couple of combs for her hair, as well as to browse down Jalan Surabaya, Jakarta's famous flea market, where she bought a pair of unusual earrings that winked and glittered in the light.

They might not make Gil fall in love with her, but at least she would have tried. She was determined to make the most of every minute she had left with him. Even if it was only for a month, let it be a month to remember.

'Where have you been?' Gil demanded the moment she let herself into the room where he had been pacing up and down. 'I thought you'd have been back hours ago. I've been worried sick about you!'

'I've been shopping,' said Deborah, her new-found optimism dissolving already in the face of his anger. She must have been mad to have even dreamt that he might fall for her. She dropped her bags on to one of the chairs, and tried to school her expression into nonchalance. He seemed so grim that she was terribly afraid that the Minister must have refused them the new contract. 'How did you get on at your meeting?' she asked.

'Fine.' Gil walked over to the window and looked broodingly down at the beautifully manicured gardens.

Deborah followed him anxiously. What did he mean, *fine*? 'Did you get the contract?'

'Oh, yes. Yes, we did.'

'You did?' Deborah threw her arms about him in spontaneous delight and kissed him on the cheek. 'Oh, Gil, I'm so pleased!'

For a second, his arms tightened hard about her, but then he dropped them, and Deborah stepped back, suddenly awkward. 'Aren't *you* pleased?'

'Of course I am.' Gil didn't quite meet her eyes. 'It's a big success for the firm. I'll be able to leave Pascal in charge here and move on to other projects as planned.' He sounded as if he was trying to convince himself. 'I've been on to the office in London this afternoon, and they say there's a chance of a development project in Madagascar if I can get out there and put in a proposal in time.'

'Madagascar?' said Deborah in a hollow voice. It seemed so far away. Gil was already planning his life without her, she realised with a renewed sense of anguish. Look at how quickly he had dropped his arms, as if he couldn't bear to touch her! What a presumptuous fool she had been to think that she could take Debbie's place! 'How exciting.'

'You probably find anywhere exciting,' he said with an odd edge.

Not without you, she wanted to cry, but she had promised herself that there would be no more arguments, no embarrassing scenes during these last few weeks. She would play it as he wanted it. Tonight she would be on her best behaviour; she wouldn't ask for more than for him to admit that she hadn't let him down.

'Yes, well, that's the joy of travelling, isn't it?' she said with a brittle smile, moving away as if casually. Let him think that she would happily carry on as before, just as he was planning to. 'Always somewhere new to see, someone new to meet. I love it,' she added, thinking dismally that she wouldn't care if she never went anywhere again.

Deborah deliberately lingered in the shower before getting dressed. She didn't want to get ready in front of Gil in case she lost her nerve and eventually he went off, muttering impatiently, to wait for their guests downstairs, after having made her promise faithfully not to be late.

It didn't take her that long to get ready once he had gone. Instead of leaving her hair loose, or plaiting it as she usually did, Deborah dried it in a silken cloud and then piled it on top of her head. Holding it up with one hand, she sucked in her cheeks and inspected herself in the mirror. It definitely made her look more sophisticated, she decided, pleased. It was a shame about the soft tendrils that kept escaping around her face, rather spoiling the elegant effect, but she couldn't do much about them.

Fixing her hair in place with the combs, she wriggled into the dress. The demureness of the mandarin collar was belied by the side-splits on the skirt, and the way the dress clung to her slender curves. For a moment, Deborah regarded herself doubtfully. It made her look alarmingly seductive, and she wasn't sure that she could live up to the image. She had never worn such a dress before, but it was too late to change her mind now, she reminded herself sternly.

She hadn't worn make-up for so long that she had almost forgotten how, but she managed to highlight her eyes quite effectively and then dabbed nervously at her cheeks with a blusher-brush. She usually ended up looking like a clown when she tried blusher, but tonight she stopped as soon as the merest hint gave delicate emphasis to her cheekbones. Lastly, she fixed in the dramatic, dangling earrings and outlined her mouth with a bold red lipstick. She was ready.

Outside the bar, she hesitated, twisting Gil's ring around her finger. What would Gil think of her? Would he like her like this? Taking a deep breath, she pushed open the door and walked in.

The tables, surrounded by exotically high-backed rattan chairs, were divided by potted palms which gave each group an air of intimacy. A piano tinkled somewhere in the background, and in spite of the air-conditioning ceiling fans circulated slowly above, presumably for effect. Deborah's heels clicked on the marble floor as she walked through, looking for Gil, oblivious to the admiring heads turning to watch her pass.

She saw him at last, sitting cool and remote at one of the tables. His eyes, light and watchful, were on the door. He must be keeping an eye out for the Seraputris, she realised, and smiled as she walked up to the table. Gil's gaze passed indifferently over her and then swivelled back, widening in shock.

'Deborah?' He got to his feet automatically, looking as if he had been punched hard in the stomach, and Deborah's nerves tightened at the look in his eyes. Her heart slowed right down and began to thud with such painfully sluggish strokes that she was afraid it would stop altogether.

'I don't look that different, do I?' she tried to say lightly, but her mouth was dry.

'Why, yes. You look...' She had never seen Gil at a loss for words before. 'You look——'

'Ah! Mr Hamilton!' A portly Indonesian dressed in the traditional batik shirt beamed at them. 'And Mrs Hamilton, I presume?'

Gil stared at him as if he wasn't sure who he was, before he managed to pull himself together with a visible effort. 'Mr Seraputri!' He made hasty introductions and they sat down awkwardly around the table.

Mrs Seraputri was as exquisitely elegant as Gil and warned, but she had a warm smile and seemed amused by the way Gil kept looking at Deborah. 'You have not been married long?' she asked Deborah, who was nearly as distracted as Gil. She was still having to concentrate on her breathing.

'No—er—no, not long.' Her eyes skittered back to Gil. She had never seen such an unguarded expression in his eyes before, and her pulse raced with a wild, soaring hope.

The evening seemed endless. Mr and Mrs Seraputri seemed oblivious to the atmosphere twanging between Gil and Deborah; either that or they were too polite to comment. They lingered over coffee, though what they found to enjoy in their disjointed conversation Deborah and Gil never knew.

Deborah tried hard. She smiled and chatted, but it was impossible to focus on anyone but Gil. She couldn't keep her eyes off him: his fingers as he crumbled a roll, the muscles in his throat as he swallowed, the clean line of his jaw as he turned to Mrs Seraputri. She ached every time she looked at his mouth and her pulse boomed in her ears.

Every now and then, Gil's eyes met hers across the table. They held an intense light that held her gaze while the rest of the world receded. As if from a great distance, she heard the chink of cutlery and the low buzz of conversation, but it was drowned out by the beating of her heart. She half expected the head waiter to come over and complain that her thundering heartbeat was disturbing the other diners.

At last Mr and Mrs Seraputri decided they must go. Gil should have urged them to stay a little longer, but instead he leapt to his feet a little too quickly. There was another agonising ten minutes in the hotel lobby while they said their goodbyes, and then, abruptly it seemed, Deborah found herself alone with Gil.

Without speaking, without touching, they walked to the lift and let it carry them silently to the third floor. She was excruciatingly aware of his body moving beside her but scared to look at him again in case the enchantment had gone. She looked at the carpet, at the numbers on the door, and when they reached their room she stared fixedly at the handle.

'You've got the key,' Gil reminded her softly.

The undercurrent of amusement in his voice was unmistakable, and Deborah burned with mortification. The enchantment *had* gone. She was behaving like a besotted schoolgirl and he was laughing at her.

'Here.' She thrust the key at him, the colour flaring in her cheeks.

The room was lit only by the soft glow of bedside lights. Deborah was convinced by now that Gil's silence was mocking. The door clicked to behind him, and she searched feverishly for something to say to fill the echoing silence. She sat down on the edge of the bed and bent her head as she busied herself taking off her shoes, willing her face not to betray the desire that swirled around her.

'I hope you thought I looked smart enough,' she said, her voice high and unnaturally sharp.

Gil didn't answer at once and as the silence lengthened Deborah glanced up. He was watching her with a smile that tightened her scalp and clenched at her heart. 'I thought you looked beautiful,' he said. He walked over to the bed and pulled an unresisting Deborah to her feet. 'You still do.' His voice was very deep and warm.

Deborah's body throbbed as he took the combs from her hair very carefully and let them drop to the floor. The silky hair tumbled to her shoulders and he took handfuls of it, rubbing it between his fingers. 'I didn't know until tonight just how beautiful you are,' he said quietly.

Her eyes were dark and dilated with desire as she stared up at him, her heart slamming painfully against her ribs. He was standing very close.

His hands slipped below the soft fall of her hair to the zip at the back of her dress. 'I've been wanting to do this all evening,' he whispered. With excruciating slowness, he slid the zip down her spine and she shivered where his fingers brushed against her skin. She wore no bra, and the lamplight caught the full curve of her breasts as the dress fell discarded to the floor.

Gil had barely touched her yet, but the knowledge of what was to come, of what could be resisted no longer, burned bright between them. There was no haste, just an exquisite, almost painful anticipation.

Deborah undid the buttons on his shirt with the same careful deliberation and when she had finished she pulled it free of his trousers so that she could spread her hands against his chest as if to convince herself that he was real. He was warm and breathing beneath her fingers and she looked up into his face and smiled.

He smiled back and the air between them tightened imperceptibly. His hands were at her waist, sliding up her nakedness, lingering possessively over her sweet curves. Deborah shuddered with pleasure beneath his touch and she arched her back sinuously against the pressure of his hard hands as she wrapped her arms around his neck.

'Deborah...' Gil's grip tightened, and he pulled her close. She sank into his kiss, excited by the rough urgency of his touch that matched her own spiralling need. Locked in his arms, her breasts pressed against the unyielding strength of his chest, and her body flamed at the gasping sensation of skin on skin.

Their kisses became deeper and more demanding and, still kissing almost frantically, they fumbled with a new desperation at the rest of their clothes as if regretting their previous lack of haste.

Deborah's senses were spinning with exhilaration and the pent-up desires of the last two months. At last she could touch him and feel him; at last his mouth was on hers and his hands were sure against her skin; at last his need was as great as her own.

The bed was pressing against the back of her knees and she sank down on to it, pulling Gil with her. They rolled over, half laughing, half desperate.

'Do you know what it's been like, sitting opposite you all evening and not being able to touch you?' Gil demanded, kissing her eyes and her ears and her throat and then her mouth again.

'I know, I know,' gasped Deborah, giving kiss for kiss and running her hands greedily over his body. 'I thought everyone in the restaurant must be able to see how much I wanted you.'

Gil rolled her beneath him and took her face in his hands, smoothing back the tousled hair. He looked into her eyes and there was such warmth in his expression that Deborah felt herself dissolve with happiness. 'Do you?' he asked softly. 'Do you really?'

Pulling his head down to hers, she breathed, 'Yes,' against his lips. The desperation faded into deep, sweet, deliberate kisses until Deborah was giddy with the spinning delight.

Gil smoothed his hands over her slenderness in wondering exploration, and his gaze lingered possessively on the soft curves of breast and hip, on the smooth, slender line of her thigh and the silken warmth of her skin. Arching beneath his touch, Deborah abandoned herself to a shivering excitement. She tried to reach for him to pull him back to her mouth, but he only smiled and continued his devastating assault on her senses by kissing her all over, slow, tantalising kisses that burned over her skin and left her sobbing with desire.

At last his mouth retraced its way back up over her stomach, teasing her taut breasts and drifting lovingly up the pure line of her throat to recapture her lips. Deborah's fingers dug into his back. She was liquid beneath him, afire with passion and a need that demanded to be fulfilled, and she welcomed him into her flooding warmth, wrapping herself around him and giving herself up to the glorious rhythm of their bodies moving together. Swept along by an irresistible force that grew ever stronger and faster and more urgent, they clung to each other with hot mouths and hungry hands.

Gil buried his face in her hair and murmured her name, and she arched her head back, beyond speaking, beyond thinking, beyond anything but feeling. He filled her, and it was as if every nerve down to the tips of her fingers thrilled with awareness of the hard, strong body that was taking her to the limits of sensation. She could feel his hands, insistent against her breasts, could taste his mouth and smell his hair and touch the sleekness of his skin, but as the rhythm grew even those senses dissolved, sucked into a spiral of shared excitement which spun faster and faster until it shattered at last in an explosion of timeless ecstasy.

CHAPTER NINE

AFTERWARDS, he held her, smoothing back her hair and gentling his hands over her skin, which still glowed with his loving. 'It's ironic that this is the first night we've had separate beds. All those weeks of lying next to you and knowing that if I reached out I could touch you, but not being able to!'

'I wish you had,' Deborah confessed, stretching like a cat beneath his tender hands.

'How could I? I'd practically blackmailed you into the pretence as it was, and I could hardly take advantage of the fact that you were forced into sharing that damned bed with me.'

She rolled herself on top of him and began pressing thoughtful little kisses along his jaw. 'I wouldn't have minded,' she murmured against his ear and his arms tightened around her once more.

'My self-control has been stretched to the limit recently,' said Gil, and she could feel him smiling. 'The double bed was bad enough, without having to share a single one at the beach that night. Can you imagine what it was like having you in my arms and knowing that it didn't affect you in the least?'

Deborah broke off from her tantalising assault and raised her head to look down at him in surprise. 'How can you say that?'

'For a start you slept like a baby and with about as much awareness of me! I know because I lay awake and stared at the ceiling all night, trying not to notice how soft and warm you were.' He grinned and tangled his fingers in her dishevelled hair. 'That was the longest night of my life! My self-control couldn't stand any more, and when you walked into the bar tonight it snapped completely. I couldn't believe that the beautiful woman walking towards me could really be you. I felt as if I'd never seen you before. Suddenly it was impossible to ignore all the things I've been trying so hard not to notice over the last few weeks, like the way you screw your face up when you're concentrating, and how warm and blue your eyes are when you smile, and how your hair catches the light sometimes when you turn your head.'

Her hair tumbled around them as he pulled her face down to his for a kiss that left Deborah dizzy with happiness.

'Gil?' she mumbled into his neck when she could talk.

'Yes?'

'You won't let your self-control get the better of you again, will you?'

Gil shook with laughter as her hands drifted luxuriously over him. 'If you carry on doing that, Deborah, it doesn't stand a chance!'

'I meant for the next few weeks.' Feeling him stiffen suddenly, Deborah hurried on, desperate not to leave him thinking that she was as pushy as Sylvie, 'I know it would just be for another month.'

'Another month?' Gil studied the ceiling, but he continued to stroke her hair mindlessly. 'Is that all it is?'

Anxious to reassure him that she had no intention of becoming an embarrassment to him, she pulled herself away slightly so that she could look at him. 'Since we're going to be sleeping in the same bed, it seems a shame not to make the most of it,' she said cajolingly. 'I couldn't bear to go back to clinging to the edge of the bed, not after tonight.'

Gil didn't reply immediately, and she wondered if she had taken too much for granted. 'It wouldn't really change anything,' she said. 'In a month's time, we'll go our separate ways, just as we agreed.'

'Yes.' Gil's voice sounded oddly flat. 'We did agree that, didn't we?'

'I'd understand if you didn't want to,' said Deborah uncertainly. 'I just thought...'

'Not want to make love to you for another month?' Gil seemed to pull himself together with an effort. 'Of course I want that!' He kissed her fiercely. 'You're right. We should make the most of the time that we've got left.'

Five days later, Deborah sat on the veranda listening to the rain crashing on to the corrugated iron roof and remembering that magical night. The nights since then had been just as enchanted.

In the office, Gil was as businesslike as ever, but every now and then, if he was standing by her chair, he would let his hand rest at the nape of her neck, or slide possessively down her spine, and their eyes would meet and smile in anticipation of the night to come. The future was never referred to, but the prospect of separation gave their lovemaking a desperate intensity and dulled the edge of Deborah's happiness.

She *was* happy, she told herself, and when Gil took her in his arms at night she was sure that she would never be happier. It was only when she was alone that the thought of living without him crept over her like a chill draught. Sometimes she wondered if it would have been better if they had never made love at all, but then she would remember the shuddering excitement of his kisses and the way his hands felt against her skin, and she knew that even a month of loving Gil would be worth the misery of a lifetime without him.

Thunder rumbled overhead and Deborah looked anxiously at her watch. She hoped Gil was all right. There was some problem with the resettlement programme for the villages in the valley to be flooded, and he had warned her that he would be late getting back, but surely he should be back by now?

Driving conditions were even worse than usual now that the monsoon had started with a vengeance. Deborah had been impressed by the rain before, but the monsoon rain was even more spectacular. The air would close and darken and then the heavens would open and the rain would crash down on to the roofs and bounce off the roads. Prim complained that she was permanently wet, but Deborah was too bound up with Gil to mind anything.

She sat up straighter as she saw some headlights coming slowly down the road. It was impossible to hear the car over the sound of the rain, but it must be Gil at last. The car stopped behind the frangipani tree and a figure ran through the wet to the shelter of the veranda. Smiling, Deborah got to her feet, but it wasn't Gil she saw with a stupid shock of disappointment.

It was Ian. He looked strained and unhappy. 'I'm sorry to come without any warning, Deborah, but I had to talk to someone,' he apologised, slicking back his wet hair nervously.

'That's all right.' Deborah pushed him into a chair and brought him a beer. 'Gil's not here at the moment.'

'I know. That's why I came.' Ian sighed and stared down at his beer. 'Gil's a good man to work for, but I'd rather not bother him with my personal problems.'

Deborah sat beside him on the rattan sofa. 'Tell me,' she said sympathetically. 'Gil doesn't need to know. Is it your girlfriend?'

'It's six weeks since I had a letter from her,' Ian burst out. 'I've written and written, but she doesn't reply. I can't believe she'd drop me without a word. I'm sure something's wrong, but I'm stuck out here and I can't do anything about it.' He took an angry gulp of his beer. 'When you were in Jakarta I asked Idja to send a telex to my father asking him to find out what was going on, but I haven't heard back yet. He could send a message any day, but Gil wants me to move up to the tunnel site tomorrow, so I won't know anything till I come back down. That could be weeks!'

'Don't worry,' said Deborah practically. 'If the message comes in, I'll contact you on the radio.'

'Would you?' His face brightened. 'At least that way I'd know one way or another. It's driving me crazy imagining the worst.'

'I'm sure everything's all right,' Deborah soothed him. She was beginning to worry about Gil, but

Ian seemed to need to talk, so she sat and listened and kept an eye out for Gil's car.

At last Ian got to his feet. 'I'm so glad you're here, Deborah. It really helps having someone to talk to, and you've been wonderful. Gil's a very lucky man.' Impulsively, he reached out and gave her a hug. 'Thank you for listening.'

'Am I interrupting something?' Gil's cold voice came from the veranda steps, and they both spun around.

Deborah knew that she looked self-conscious and guilty. 'I didn't hear you come up,' she said, trying not to sound flustered. 'The rain's so loud you can't hear anything.'

'Perhaps you weren't expecting me quite yet?' he said unpleasantly, coming up the last step of the veranda, and Deborah quailed at the expression in his light, angry eyes.

'We've been waiting for you,' she tried to explain. 'Ian's been keeping me company.'

'So I see.'

'I was just saying to Deborah that you're a lucky man to have her,' Ian tried in a hearty voice, but he got no encouragement from Gil.

'Were you?' he said between his teeth.

Ian glanced nervously from Gil to Deborah. 'Well—er—I'd better be going. Thanks again, Deborah.' He ran down the path to his car and was quickly swallowed up by the rain.

'Did you have to be quite so rude?' Deborah demanded as soon as he had gone.

'Did you have to snuggle up to him like that?' Gil retorted. 'I didn't think you'd be quite that quick off the mark to take advantage of my absence!'

Deborah's lips tightened. 'You know perfectly well I wasn't doing anything of the kind! Ian just wanted someone to talk to. He's worried about something.'

'If he's that worried he can come and talk to me.'

'You wouldn't understand,' she said helplessly.

'I can understand all right when I come home and find him with his arms around you!' Gil let the screen door slam behind him as he went inside, and refused point blank to discuss the matter any further when Deborah tried again to explain.

She gave up in the end, but she was too angry to speak to him after that, and they spent the evening in hostile silence which lasted until the next morning. They lay stiffly at the edges of the bed with their backs pointedly turned towards each other.

It was all so stupid, Deborah thought miserably the next morning as she unlocked the office. Gil had gone off with Deden to meet the local re-settlement officer with barely a word to her. He wouldn't listen to her when she tried to tell him about Ian, and she was damned if she was going to apologise for nothing. It was all his fault for being pigheaded and unreasonable!

She felt tired and headachy all morning. It was just as well that Gil wasn't there, she thought, listlessly photocopying a report. She couldn't concentrate on anything and the drumming sound of the rain on the roof was making her headache worse.

'You look pale,' Idja said. 'Why don't you go home?'

What was there to go home to if Gil wasn't there? Suddenly Deborah felt tears very close. 'I'm all right,' she said gruffly. In the corner, the telex machine chattered and she went over to it, glad of the diversion.

'Bad news?' asked Idja, watching Deborah's face as she bent over to read the message.

'It's for Ian.' Deborah tore off the message and re-read it thoughtfully. 'He's been worried about not hearing from his girlfriend, but apparently she's been in hospital—a car accident, it says here. She's out of danger, thank goodness. His father says she didn't tell Ian because she didn't want to worry him! The poor man's been beside himself!' She gave Idja the message to read and picked up the radio. 'I promised I'd let him know as soon as any news came through,' she explained, but although she tried for some time it was impossible to get through to the tunnel site and all they heard was the crackle of static.

'It's always difficult getting through during the monsoon,' said Idja. 'It'll have to wait until he comes back to base.'

'That might not be for some time, and he's desperate to know.' Deborah glanced outside where the rain had stopped at last. 'I could drive up to the tunnel camp and leave the message for him. We're not too busy at the moment, and I wouldn't mind getting out for a bit.'

'The track will be very wet,' Idja said doubtfully.

'I'll be careful.' The more she thought about it, the more Deborah liked the idea. She needed some time on her own and the fresh air might do her headache some good. Besides, she had promised

Ian that she would let him know as soon as possible, and even if they did get through on the radio the static would be so bad he might easily misunderstand the message. 'It only takes an hour to get there, so I should easily be back before you leave.'

She took the office pick-up. Gil had taken her up to the tunnel once, and the track was easy to follow, but she had only been going about ten minutes when there was an enormous thunderclap above her and she was enveloped in another downpour. The windscreen wipers slapped frantically as she edged her way forward and her confidence rapidly evaporated. As Idja had warned, the track was dangerously slippy in places and in other parts it was hard to find a way through without bogging down in the thick red mud.

Instead of lessening, Deborah's headache got steadily worse until it was an iron band gripping her brain, and her hands were slippery on the steering-wheel. She clung to it determinedly. She would get the message to Ian and then she would go home to bed, but she didn't want to think what the return journey down the hillside would be like.

Peering through the windscreen, her aching eyes suddenly focused on a yawning gap in the road, and she stamped on the brake so that the pick-up skidded horribly in the mud. She was shaking as she got out of the cab, heedless of the rain.

The road had simply disappeared. The relentless downpours had loosened a weak section of the soil, and it had slid down the steep hillside below, taking the track with it. Deborah peeked cautiously over the edge and shuddered at the vertiginous drop. There was no possible way she could go forward, and she had no intention of trying to turn the pick-up round, not with that drop and the treacherously slippy mud.

Deborah's knees began to shake again as the reality of her situation hit her. Why hadn't she listened to Idja? She got back into the cab and held her aching head between her hands, trying to think sensibly. She had no idea how far she had come. It felt like miles, but she had been going very slowly most of the time, so it might not be that far. She longed to be back in the house, but the only way she was going to get there was to walk. She had no jacket and unsuitable shoes, and she looked out at the rain, wondering how she could ever have liked it.

Forcing herself into action, she took the torch she found in the glove compartment and began to trudge back the way she had come. She was sodden in a matter of seconds, but after a while the rain ceased to matter. Her head hurt so badly that it was all she could do to put one foot in front of another, and she slipped frequently in the mud, dragging herself to her feet by sheer effort of will.

Deborah lost track of time as she slithered down the track, and the gathering darkness only added to her misery. She was shivering violently and her legs became more and more unsteady as the ache in her head spread over her body.

Suddenly, she tripped again. It took a little time to register that she had fallen against something, but she managed to get herself up, trembling, and flashed the torch. There had been another landslide, this time from above, and the track was completely blocked by the muddy debris. Deborah had never felt more like giving up. She knew that it wasn't that high a climb, but in her weakened state it looked like Mount Everest. She looked down at her hands as if they could summon up some extra energy, and it was then that she realised that her ring was missing. It could have come off at any one of the times she had fallen. In a matter of weeks, that ring might have been all that she had to remember Gil by, and now she would never see it again.

For Deborah, it was the last straw. She burst into tears. Still sobbing bitterly and hardly aware of what she was doing, she began to clamber up the landslide. When she heard her name being called, she staggered to a halt and the torch wavered drunkenly, but she couldn't see anything, and the only sound was the rain. She must have imagined it.

Deborah wiped the rain out of her eyes with the back of her hand. She couldn't seem to stop crying.

'Deborah!'

The voice seemed so real that she looked around wildly, and then, suddenly, there was Gil, scrabbling frantically up the mud to reach her. She dropped the torch and practically fell down the slope in a headlong rush towards him.

Gil caught her and his arms closed around her so tightly that she couldn't breathe, and Deborah clung to his warm, reassuringly solid strength, terrified that he might disappear as unexpectedly as he had arrived.

'Are you hurt?' he demanded hoarsely, patting her all over like a dog to reassure himself.

She shook her head against his shoulder. 'I've lost my ring,' was all she could say.

'It doesn't matter about the ring.'

'It does!' she sobbed. 'I'll never find it again.'

In spite of his comforting warmth, she was still shivering uncontrollably, and Gil felt her forehead with an exclamation.

'You're burning up! Come on, let's get you off this damned mud.' He half carried her down to where his car had been stopped by the landslide and bundled her inside before turning the car round with a skill that Deborah would have envied if she had been in any state to care. She felt too ill to do anything more than slump unprotestingly while Gil wrapped a blanket around her and pulled her across the seat so that she lay with her head on his thigh. His presence burned clear and comforting through the fever, and she clutched the blanket around her shoulders as she burrowed into him, knowing that he would look after her.

Later she thought that it must have been a ghastly drive for Gil, down the treacherous track in the torrential rain, with a sick girl beside him, but at the time she was aware only of his hand resting firmly on her shoulder.

She was delirious by the time they reached the house. Gil carried her inside and stripped her of her sodden clothes before laying her in the double bed and tucking her up with blankets. Surfacing briefly, she saw his face, tight with worry, leaning over her.

'I'm going to get Prim,' he said.

She didn't want Prim, Deborah thought feverishly. She only wanted him.

They told her later that she was delirious for two days. It was all a blur to Deborah. All she could remember was calling out for Gil and feeling him grip her hand firmly and his calm voice saying, 'I'm here.' She would cling to his hand and try and tell him about Ian and losing the ring, but the words never seemed to come out properly and she would drift back into delirium.

When the fever finally broke, Deborah woke to see Prim's smiling face.

'Gil?' she croaked.

Prim grinned and rolled her eyes. 'Yes, yes, he's here! He's hardly left your side for a moment. Trust you to come round the very moment I sent him off to get some more water. I'll get him for you.' She went to the door and called for him, and Gil appeared a few seconds later, pushing past her when he saw that Deborah was awake.

Prim took herself tactfully away as he sat on the edge of the bed and took Deborah's hand.

'Hello,' she said weakly.

'How are you feeling?'

'Awful,' she said, and he smiled.

'You look ten times better than you did, if that's any comfort. I was lucky I found you when I did. You'd never have made it back down by yourself.'

'You mean you were looking for me?'

'Of course I was!' Gil pushed the damp hair away from her forehead. 'I spent that day feeling terrible about that stupid argument we had, and as soon as I could get away from the resettlement officer I went to the office. I was going to apologise to you and admit that I'd been stupidly jealous, but when I got there Idja was looking worried. She told me you'd insisted on going up to see Ian with some message.'

'I promised him I'd let him know as soon as there was any news about his girlfriend,' Deborah whispered. She felt too tired to talk, but she was desperate to explain. 'I thought he ought to know that she'd been in hospital as soon as he could.'

'I know that now,' said Gil with a wry look. 'Ian's on his way home to see her at this very moment. I even apologised to him for being curt, and he told me how kind you'd been. He told me again that I was a lucky man and this time I didn't bite his head off!'

'I don't suppose you felt very lucky when you were driving up that track in the rain.'

His hand tightened around hers. 'I was lucky to find you at all. I was furious when Idja told me where you'd gone. I thought you'd rushed off at the first excuse to see Ian, but when I knew you were on the track in that rain my blood ran cold. We managed to raise the tunnel site on the radio, and they told us they hadn't seen you, by which time I was frantic and determined to set out after you. When I got to that landslide, I kept imagining all the dreadful things that might have happened to you.' He looked away from Deborah's white face to the wall where a gecko froze in mid-scuttle as if aware of his eyes. 'I can't tell you how I felt when you came staggering over the top of the landslide. I must have used up a lifetime of luck in that moment.'

'I'm sorry,' whispered Deborah. 'I've been such a lot of trouble for you.'

Gil's smile was warm as he reached out and flicked her cheek tenderly with his finger. 'You've been trouble ever since you fell off that bus,

Deborah! Now you're going to have to do as you're told for once, and get better quickly.'

She slept for most of the next few days, but whenever she woke Gil was there. Prim came in regularly to take her temperature and check that her patient was doing well, but it was Gil who really nursed her. He washed her face and changed her sheets and bullied Sarmi into cooking special meals which he thought would tempt her appetite. During the day he sat at a table in the room and worked on his papers while she dozed, and at night he slept on the camp bed that someone had brought in for him, ready to get up if she stirred.

Deborah opened her eyes one morning feeling immeasurably better. The camp bed was empty, and she could hear Gil talking to Sarmi in the kitchen. Gingerly, she swung her legs out of bed and tottered to the bathroom. Her bones felt as if they were made of cotton wool, and just getting to the door was a major effort, but she felt better still when she had washed her face and brushed her teeth.

Gil caught her as she was on her way back to bed. 'What do you think you're doing out of bed?' he said sternly, putting down the cup of tea he was carrying.

'I thought I'd have a wash,' said Deborah, hanging on to the back of a chair.

'You're too weak to be gadding around by yourself,' he said, straightening the sheets and plumping up her pillows. 'Get back into bed at once.'

Deborah felt as if she would never gad anywhere again as she gratefully sank back against the pillows.

'You only gad around somewhere exciting. You can't gad to the bathroom.'

Gil sat down on the edge of the bed. 'You must be feeling better if you're answering back! Here.' He handed her the cup of tea. 'Drink this. Prim says you're to have plenty of liquids.'

'You've got enough to do without waiting on me,' said Deborah, sipping obediently at her tea. 'What's happening at the office?'

'We're surviving without you,' Gil said drily. 'It's uncannily quiet without you chattering all day, but I suspect a lot more work is being done. Deden and Idja sit around like lost souls at lunchtime. They both send their love and say that they're missing you.'

'How is Idja coping with all the typing? She must be doing all my work as well as her own.'

Gil hesitated. 'I've arranged for her to have some help. Sylvie comes in in the mornings to help out.'

'Oh,' said Deborah jealously, hating the thought of Sylvie in her place. 'She must be enjoying being indispensable again!'

'I don't think she realised that I'd be spending quite so much time here,' said Gil, and although he was straight-faced his eyes gleamed with quiet amusement. 'By the time she found out that I was chained to your bedside, it was too late for her to refuse to help Idja.'

Deborah laughed. 'It's Idja I feel sorry for. Tell her that I'll be back soon.'

'I'll tell her nothing of the kind.'

'But Gil, I feel so much better!'

'You're not going back to work at all.' He took the empty cup from her hand. 'We're due to leave in less than two weeks, and you certainly won't be well enough to go to work before then.'

Leaving. Deborah's eyes darkened at the thought. 'I suppose you've found out that Sylvie is a much better secretary than I am!'

'I always knew that,' said Gil, putting the cup on the table and turning back to take her hands. 'You're not jealous, are you, Deborah?' he teased.

Deborah's fingers curled round his and he lifted each hand in turn to plant a kiss in her palm. 'No,' she said huskily.

Her eyes met his almost shyly. He was smiling, his pale eyes alight with warmth, and he leant forward and kissed her mouth, a long, sweet kiss that set Deborah's heart singing.

'How's the patient today? Oh, sorry——!' Prim broke off as she bustled into the room and saw Deborah melting into Gil's embrace. 'Obviously feeling much better!' she grinned as they broke apart almost guiltily and, to her chagrin, Deborah realised that she was blushing.

'I really think you could go to work today,' Prim went on firmly as Gil got to his feet with some reluctance, 'The whole project is grinding to a halt waiting for you to make various decisions and poor Pascal is running round in circles. I'll look after Deborah till you get back.'

CHAPTER TEN

PRIM shooed Gil out of the room. 'I've never seen anything distract him from his work before,' she said to Deborah with a hint of awe. 'Things aren't that bad, of course, but it'll do him good to go back to work and stop worrying about you for a few hours. He's been frantic.' She shook a thermometer with a professional air and stuck it in Deborah's mouth. 'I told him it was just a tropical fever and that you'd sweat yourself out of it in the end, but he was all for airlifting you back to London! As it was, he hardly left your side for a moment. You kept calling for him when you were delirious and mumbling about some ring you'd lost.'

Deborah had forgotten about losing her ring, but as she looked down at her bare finger she was overwhelmed with sadness again, and she remembered what Gil had said about leaving. Less than two weeks; that was all the time they had left.

As she removed the thermometer, Prim noticed Deborah's eyes fill with tears. 'You'd better rest,' she said kindly. 'You're still very weak.'

If she hadn't been so aware of time running out, Deborah would have enjoyed her convalescence. Everyone—with the notable exception of Sylvie—seemed to find time to pop in and keep her company for a few minutes, and when there was no one to talk to she would curl up on the sofa and watch

Sarmi, whose graceful, unhurried presence was strangely soothing. She would stoop as she swept the floor, one hand resting in the small of her back, and the broom would swish quietly from side to side in a slow, hypnotic rhythm.

But most of all Deborah waited for Gil to come home. They would sit over their meal, talking, or sometimes they would play Scrabble and Gil would never let her win, even though the rest of the time he insisted on treating her like a fragile invalid. He was very strict about making her go to bed early, and, to her increasing frustration, he continued to sleep on the narrow, uncomfortable camp bed.

With less than a week to go, Deborah decided to take matters into her own hands. She brushed out her hair and found a couple of candles to put on the table. She changed into a clean sarong and went outside to pick a spray of frangipani to put in her hair. Standing under the tree, she breathed in its heady perfume and remembered how Gil had kissed her there. She hungered for the hard demand of his body and the passionate delight of his kisses. She didn't want to be kissed like an invalid. She wanted him to kiss her as if he loved her and needed her the same way she loved and needed him.

After they had eaten, and Gil had gone to sit in his usual chair, Deborah got up without a word and slid on to his lap. She slipped her arms about his neck and trailed soft kisses along his jaw to the cool, firm mouth that burned in her memory when he was gone.

'What are you doing, Deborah?' Gil asked huskily, unable to resist running a hand over her thigh.

Deborah's lips brushed tantalisingly over his and then continued their slow, delicious exploration to his other earlobe. 'I'm seducing you,' she murmured against the pulse that beat below his ear.

'I thought you were ill,' said Gil, but his hands slid up of their own accord to tangle in her hair, and the frangipani fell unheeded to the floor as he held her head still for longer, deeper kisses.

'I'm better now.'

He lifted her up and carried her to bed where he made love to her with a sweetness and a passion that made Deborah cry out in ecstasy and left her lying in his arms, warm and replete with happiness.

She was still cocooned in contentment when Sylvie came to see her the next day, but it began to fade as soon as the Frenchwoman walked through the door. She had a sly, spiteful look about her that made Deborah stiffen in instant distrust.

'You don't look very ill to me,' said Sylvie after a perfunctory greeting. She eyed Deborah's glowing face with suspicion. 'I suppose you were bored with playing at being Gil's secretary and decided that you might as well let me finish your work?'

'Of course not,' Deborah protested.

'No? Then perhaps you are getting bored with playing at being Gil's wife?'

There was a frozen pause. 'What on earth do you mean?' said Deborah at last.

'You're not married to Gil, are you?' Sylvie gave a tinkling laugh. 'I should have guessed. Gil's hardly likely to commit himself to someone like you, after all.'

'We are married,' Deborah said doggedly.

'Oh, no, you're not. One of your jobs that I've been doing is checking the telex for messages,' Sylvie explained with sinister sweetness. 'And guess what message came in the other day?'

'How should I know?'

'I'll let you read it, shall I?' Sylvie flicked the piece of paper contemptuously over to Deborah, who caught it as it fluttered to the floor. It was addressed to Gil from his office in London.

BEST CONGRATULATIONS ON YOUR FORTHCOMING MARRIAGE TO DEBRA CLARK STOP WILL MAKE ARRANGEMENTS AS REQUESTED FOR HER TO TRAVEL WITH YOU TO MADAGASCAR STOP PLEASE INFORM SOONEST OF WEDDING DATE SO CAN BOOK FLIGHTS ACCORDINGLY.

'Rather an odd message to a man who is supposedly already married, don't you think?' said Sylvie, but Deborah hardly heard her. She was staring down at the message in her hand.

Debra Clark.

The name wavered in front of her eyes. Debra, not Deborah. Clark, not Clarke. It wasn't her. They weren't talking about her. It was Debbie he was planning to marry, not her. A cold hand closed about her heart, cutting off all feeling and leaving her curiously numb.

He had lied to her. He had told her that he had written to Debbie to tell her they were no longer engaged, and all the time he had been carrying on with his plans for the future. Had he lied to Debbie as well? Had he persuaded her to marry him after all, conveniently forgetting to mention that he was living with a gullible little fool who was prepared to take whatever he could give?

With a supreme effort, Deborah forced a smile. At least Sylvie didn't realise that the telex didn't refer to her. 'So we're not really married. What difference does it make?'

'He won't marry you this time either,' Sylvie said viciously. 'Oh, I know why he did it! He brought you here as a show, because he was afraid of his own feelings for me. I suspected that he was trying to disguise the fact that he was in love with me, but it was obvious really. He asked me to help in the office so he could be near me and he seized every opportunity to be alone with me whenever Pascal was away.' She shrugged in a way that only a Frenchwoman could. 'Perhaps I encouraged him a little too much, but he can be very attractive, and sometimes I was lonely, too.'

Deborah's throat was closed and her mouth felt stiff. 'If he was so much in love with you, why is he planning to marry me?'

'Because he knows that he can never marry me,' Sylvie said promptly. 'I suppose he thinks that if he can't have me he might as well marry anyone, but he will soon get bored with a naïve little idiot like you.'

'You don't know what you're talking about,' said Deborah, who was beginning to shake with anger and the bitter effort of not crying. 'I don't believe a word of what you're saying. Gil has never been in love with you.' Or had he? a bitter voice whispered inside her. Had his story about Sylvie's persistence been a lie too? 'If you must know,' she went on, pushing the thought aside, 'he found your rather obvious attempts to seduce him distasteful and embarrassing, and if it hadn't been for his relationship with Pascal he would have told you so himself.' Somehow she walked over to the screen door and opened it. 'Now I think you'd better go.'

Sylvie stalked past her, her dark eyes blazing. 'Your marriage will never last!' she spat venomously, but Deborah simply shut the door in her face without deigning to reply and Sylvie had no choice but to leave. Deborah heard her heels clattering angrily down the steps, then the slam of a car door, followed by the squeal of protesting tyres as she took off at speed.

The ensuing silence echoed eerily. Deborah leant weakly against the door with her eyes squeezed shut while the comforting everyday sounds filtered back into her consciousness: the rusty squeak of the fan, the gentle swish of the *pembantu*'s broom on the next-door veranda, the haunting cry of the orange-seller at the end of the road.

Gil was going to marry Debbie. The thought pounded in her head. After the joy they had found together, he was still going to marry Debbie, sensible, practical Debbie, the kind of girl he had said all along that he wanted to marry.

If only he hadn't lied to her! Why had he pretended to reject Debbie's offer to patch up the engagement? Was it just an excuse to make love to her? He *had* wanted her, the last few nights had shown her that, but he had never mentioned love. He had used her, she realised with a bitterness that was a deep, physical ache. When they left Terawati, he would go back to Debbie and the efficient, emotionless future he had chosen for himself, and he wouldn't give her another thought.

When Gil came home that evening, she was sitting as usual on the veranda, flicking through a magazine Prim had lent her.

'Hello,' he said, ruffling her hair, and she nearly cried out at his touch. 'Sorry I'm a bit late, but Pascal wanted a chat.'

'What about?' she asked without much interest.

'About Sylvie. She's gone.'

'Gone?'

Gil nodded and sat down in the chair next to her. 'Apparently she told Pascal she refused to stay here a moment longer and insisted on driving down to Parang tonight. Pascal has no idea what brought on such a tantrum, but he confessed that he was glad to get rid of her. He was besotted with her at first, but she hadn't been out here long before he began to realise he'd made a disastrous mistake. So she's gone back to France.'

'Oh,' said Deborah, and Gil looked at her in concern.

'You're looking tired. What have you been up to?'

'Oh, nothing much.' Deborah kept her head bent over the magazine. 'I've been planning my trip to Australia.'

Gil stilled. 'Australia?'

'Yes. With all this money I've been earning, I should be able to do quite a bit of travelling before I have to get another job.'

There was a long pause. Deborah couldn't look at Gil so she stared blindly down at an article about the problems involved in loving two men at the same time. Loving one was problem enough for her.

'I'd forgotten that you were going to Australia,' Gil said finally. His voice sounded dead.

'Had you?' Deborah asked with jarring brightness. 'What did you think that I was going to do with all this money you've been paying me for being here?'

'I've booked two tickets to London,' he said in the same lifeless tone. 'I thought . . .' He trailed off. 'I thought you wouldn't be well enough to carry on travelling,' he finished at last.

Deborah's fingers clenched on the magazine. Suddenly she wanted to go home more than anything. She wasn't sure if she'd ever want to travel again. 'I don't mind going to London if you've got the ticket for me,' she said. To her horror her voice cracked with strain and she tried to cover it with a cough. 'It probably would be best to convalesce for a bit longer. I'll go home.'

A vision of the square stone house and the clean Northumberland air rose before her. Her father would be grumbling about greenfly on his roses and her mother would be in the kitchen, peering anxiously into the oven. Never had Deborah wanted her mother so much.

She stumbled to her feet as the tears choked her. 'I think I'll go back to bed,' she muttered. 'I don't feel very well again.'

Gil slept on the camp bed that night, accepting her excuse of a relapse without question. He was probably glad of the chance to wind down the passion before he went back to Debbie, Deborah thought desolately as she lay alone and numb with misery in the big, empty bed, and the tears trickled slowly and silently down her cheeks.

Prim was concerned at Deborah's apathy, but Gil barely spoke to her. They struggled through the last few days, both glad of the excuse of Deborah's illness to avoid the usual farewell festivities. Prim and Idja both wept when it came to say goodbye, but Deborah's heart was too tight with despair to cry any more and she could only cling to them with a dry-eyed desperation.

Deden drove them down to Parang with Deborah's shabby rucksack hidden in one of Gil's suitcases. As the camp disappeared back into the jungle, Deborah felt as if she was being torn away from the brief, intense happiness she had known with Gil. Her control nearly broke when they passed the roadside restaurant for the last time, and Deden's warm hug as he said goodbye was as much as she could bear. The tears seeped down her face as they stood and watched him drive off back to Terawati, back to the friends she had made, back to the little house with its creaking fan and the big bed where Gil had made love to her and never would again.

The flight back to London seemed endless. Deborah sat by the window and clutched her hands together at take-off, but Gil made no move to reassure her as he had done before. Instead he stared ahead at the cabin, his expression grim and unhappy for a man going home to his own wedding.

Deborah sat next to him silently and tried not to look at him. The seats were so close together that it was impossible to avoid their arms and legs brushing together occasionally, but every time they

touched they would both flinch away as if afraid
of the contact. Once she succumbed to sheer
exhaustion and fell asleep, only to find herself
lolling against his shoulder when she awoke, and
she jerked herself away to lean against the window,
as far away from him as possible.

They hardly spoke until the plane began its de-
scent into Heathrow. Then Gil flipped down the
table in front of him and took out his cheque-book.
'This should settle our account,' he said in a hard
voice, handing her a cheque. 'I think you'll find it
easily covers the cost of another ticket to Australia,
so you'll end up with a tidy profit.'

Deborah looked at the cheque with loathing. She
was being paid off like any other unwanted em-
ployee. Did the sweetness and the laughter they had
shared come down to no more than this? Did Gil
really think that a sum of money made up for the
nights she would lie alone, aching for him?

Too tired and heartsore to argue, she took the
cheque without a word. If it made him feel better
to 'settle his account', she would take it, but she
would tear it up later. She didn't want his money;
she didn't want anything if she couldn't have him.

Deborah's eyes felt gritty and her jaw was
clenched with the effort of not crying as they waited
by the carousel for their bags to appear. Her
rucksack looked limp and shabby as they went
towards Customs. Too soon, they were through and
walking round the screens into a blur of happy, expectant faces and people hugging each other in
delight.

This was it. Deborah felt sick and cold. Gil was
going to turn and say goodbye and she would never

see him again, and because she couldn't bear to wait
for him to say it she got in first.

'Well . . . goodbye.'

Gil looked drawn, as desperate as she. 'Deborah,'
he said urgently and put out a hand, but before he
could finish an immaculately pretty blonde girl had
pushed her way through the crowd and had thrown
her arms around him.

'Surprise!'

He tried to step back but she wouldn't let him
go. 'I know you weren't expecting me, but I asked
your personnel people to tell me when your flight
was due so I could come and meet you.'

'Debbie,' Gil said flatly.

'Yes, it's me! Don't say you didn't recognise me!
I had to see you at once so that I could tell
you——'

Deborah didn't wait to hear Debbie tell Gil how
much she loved him. Grabbing her rucksack off the
trolley, she turned and stumbled across the con-
course, pushing her way through the throng,
heedless of the aggrieved looks that followed her
clumsy progress.

'Deborah!' she heard Gil shout after her, but she
didn't turn. She couldn't bear to see him with
Debbie.

Somehow she got herself home to
Northumberland where she was welcomed with a
delighted surprise that turned to concern when they
saw how thin and strained she was. Deborah told
them she had been ill, but her parents were clearly
unconvinced that that was the only reason. She
thought about Gil constantly, and tortured herself

by imagining him with Debbie, kissing *her*, holding *her*, loving *her*.

She struggled through the first few days and then decided to take herself to the sea to try and blow some of the black misery away. She drove to Bamburgh and walked down below the castle on to the long, wide beach. It was a beautiful day, with a high, pale blue sky and a wind that blew her hair about her face. The air was crisp and diamond-bright as she trudged with bent head along the sand. It could not have been more of a contrast to Terawati, and yet the sounds and scents of Indonesia were more vivid to her than the salt on the air or the screech of the wheeling gulls above her head. If she closed her eyes, she could still hear the whirr of insects in the darkness, or the deafening crash of rain on the iron roof, or smell the frangipani drifting through the hot, damp air.

When she could walk no further, Deborah sat on a rock and gazed out to Lindisfarne. The sea was a dark blue flecked with white waves and the sky seemed to stretch forever. With a twisted smile, she remembered the story she had made up about Gil's proposal here. She had been so light-hearted then! He had been furious, of course, but really it had all been a game, a game that should never have been allowed to become something more than that. It was her own fault for falling in love with him, Deborah admitted to herself. He hadn't fallen in love with her. All she had had to do was keep playing the game until the end, and she wouldn't have been sitting here with the gulls and the wind for company, alone except for a solitary figure walking towards her along the shoreline.

Deborah glanced at the man without interest, then she looked again. There was something familiar about the walk, wasn't there? As she watched, the figure came steadily closer and suddenly she stood up, thinking it might be easier to breathe.

She covered her eyes with her hands, terribly afraid that it was just a cruel trick of her imagination, but when she risked a glimpse through her fingers wild, incredulous hope surged through her.

The same purposeful stride, the same set of the head. It was Gil. It *had* to be Gil.

As if in a dream, Deborah slowly began to walk to meet him, but as his features became clearer her walk became faster and faster until she was running, and then he was running too. Gil swept her off her feet into his arms as they met in a breathless embrace at last, and they clung together, kissing frantically as if the other would disappear if they stopped.

'You've put me through hell trying to track you down,' Gil muttered into her hair. 'Why did you run off without letting me know where I could find you?'

'I didn't think you'd want to find me.'

'Not want to find you?' He held her so tightly that she could hardly breathe. 'How was I going to get through the rest of my life unless I *did* find you?'

'I thought you wanted to spend your life with Debbie,' Deborah said, clinging to him, still dazed at the wonder of his presence.

'I haven't wanted anything to do with Debbie since she threw up her hands in horror when I showed her some photographs of Terawati. I knew then that I'd never loved her, and that she had never really loved me either.'

'But you told me you wanted a sensible wife,' she said, tipping back her head to look up into his face.

'I did—at least, I thought I did. But then I started to fall in love with a girl who fell off a bus in front of me and was very far from sensible.' Gil took Deborah's face in his hands. 'I tried very hard not to, Deborah. I knew you enjoyed your life far too much to consider throwing in your lot with me, so I told myself that someone like Debbie would make a much more suitable wife. It helped my pride to pretend that she was the one I really wanted, when it was so obvious that you would never want to settle down with me. I reminded myself endlessly about my mother and how exasperating she could be, and I told myself that you would be just the same, but it didn't make any difference. You danced into my heart and there was no way I could get you out. You were always such fun, you brightened a room just by walking into it, and I got more and more jealous when I thought you were sharing yourself with other people. I wanted to keep you all to myself, and knowing that you were gaily planning to carry on travelling without me just made things worse.'

'I wasn't,' said Deborah, slipping her arms beneath his jacket and quivering with pleasure at the feel of his body so close to hers. 'I was just pretending that life would be worth living without you.'

Gil kissed her at that, and his eyes when he lifted his head were so warm with love that Deborah's heart felt as if it would burst. 'Are you really in love with me, Deborah?'

'Hopelessly,' she said happily, resting her cheek against his chest. 'I thought it was painfully obvious.'

'Sometimes when I held you in my arms you were so warm and vibrant and loving that I thought you must do, but then you would turn round and remind me that it was only for a few weeks and then you would be going your own way. After that first night in Jakarta, I was ready to beg you to marry me, and I felt as if I'd been kicked in the stomach when you coolly suggested that we simply make the most of the time we had left. I couldn't believe that night had meant so little to you, but I was prepared to take whatever you would give. Then you were ill, and nothing mattered except that you get better. I was going to ask you to marry me, and I even went down to Terawati to buy you another ring, but when I came back you were talking about Australia again, and you were so cold and withdrawn that I gave up. I was hurt and angry with myself for getting so involved when I knew there was no future in it.'

Deborah pulled away slightly. 'But I don't understand... Why did you tell your office you were going to marry Debbie? Sylvie showed me the telex they sent you in reply. She just wanted to prove that she knew we weren't really married, and she didn't realise that it wasn't me they were talking about at all. The telex was definitely about Debra Clark. I thought that *you* were planning to carry on without *me*.'

'So that's why you changed so suddenly! I wondered why I hadn't had an acknowledgement from the office. Those idiots in Personnel must have got the spelling wrong. I was so sure of you that I sent them a telex when you were ill asking them to make arrangements for you to come to Madagascar with me. I suppose since Debbie used to work there they thought I meant her—as if I'd get my own wife's name wrong!'

'But why did she come to the airport?'

'She wanted to tell me that she'd just got engaged to her new boss.' Gil sighed. 'She didn't want me to come home having changed *my* mind and then be hurt if I heard the news from someone else. It was a fair enough thought, I suppose, but I could cheerfully have throttled her when I saw you running off!' His arms tightened around Deborah. 'I managed to convince her in the end that I was delighted for her, and we agreed that we were both relieved that we hadn't got married. I didn't tell her, of course, but I used to wake up in a cold sweat next to you, thinking what my life would have been like if she had accepted me the first time. I would never have met you, never have known what it was like to love you.'

He grinned down into her face. 'You're exactly the kind of girl I always swore I'd never marry, Deborah. You've turned my life upside-down and ruined my reputation as a serious engineer, but I really, absolutely cannot live without you now. I spent the whole of the flight home planning how I could persuade you to come with me to Madagascar, and then you ran off before I had a chance to find out where you lived.'

He put his arm round her and they began walking slowly back along the beach. 'How *did* you find me?' asked Deborah, awash with happiness.

'Sheer perseverance,' he said. 'I knew your parents lived in this area, so I came up and started ringing every Clarke I could find in the phone book, asking if they knew you, knew where you were. Have you ever counted how many Clarkes there are round here? Seventy-one!'

Deborah began to giggle. 'My father's name's William, too. He must be right at the end!'

'Sixty-ninth, to be precise. I explained who I was and that I'd met you in Indonesia, and your mother said that if I was the reason you'd been looking as if your heart was breaking I was to come and find you at once. She gave me very specific directions, too!'

'This has always been one of my favourite places,' Deborah said.

'Is that why you chose it for my fictional proposal?'

'Yes.' She peeped a look at him. 'I always thought it would be very romantic to be proposed to here.'

He grinned. 'Do I have to wait until it's raining, or will a beautiful, sunny day do?'

'Now will do,' she said demurely.

'In that case...' Gil stopped and turned her to face him. 'Will you marry me, Deborah, and come with me to Madagascar and carry on driving me to distraction?'

'Yes,' said Deborah, 'I will,' and she kissed him.

He was smiling as he let her go. 'Since we've already been married for three months, I don't think we need to bother with an engagement, do you?

We'll just get married—properly.' Reaching into his pocket, he brought out a twist of tatty newspaper. 'They're not very hot on wrapping in Terawati market,' he explained as he unfolded the paper to produce a ring in the same dull gold as before. 'This isn't an engagement-ring, it's another wedding-ring. I thought we should keep things the same as they were.'

'Exactly the same? Does that mean I still get paid?' Deborah asked innocently, and Gil pulled her back into his arms.

'Perhaps you're right. We should negotiate a new agreement.' He pretended to consider. 'How about this? Instead of three months, you agree to marry me for a lifetime, and in return I promise to love you and cherish you and rescue you from all your predicaments. Does that sound fair?'

Deborah's eyes shone as she kissed him. 'It's a deal,' she said.

HARLEQUIN ROMANCE®

brings you

Stories that celebrate love, families and children!

Watch for our next Kids & Kisses title in November!

Who's Holding the Baby?
by Day Leclaire
Harlequin Romance #3338

Everybody loves this baby—but who's supposed to be looking after her? A delightful and very funny romance from the author of To Catch a Ghost *and* Once A Cowboy....

Toni's only three months old, and already she needs a scorecard to keep track of the people in her life! She's been temporarily left with her uncle Luc, who's recruited his secretary Grace, who's pretending to be his fiancée, hoping to mollify the police, who've called the child-welfare people, who believe that Grace and Luc are married! And then life starts to get *really* complicated....

Available wherever Harlequin books are sold.

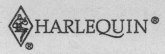

HARLEQUIN®

Weddings, Inc.

EDGE OF ETERNITY
Jasmine Cresswell

Two years after their divorce, David Powell
and Eve Graham met again in Eternity,
Massachusetts—and this time there was magic
between them. But David was tied up in a
murder that no amount of small-town gossip
could free him from. When Eve was pulled into
the frenzy, he knew he had to come up with
some answers—including how to convince her
they should marry again...this time for keeps.

EDGE OF ETERNITY, available in
November from Intrigue, is the sixth book in
Harlequin's exciting new cross-line series,
WEDDINGS, INC.

Be sure to look for the final book, **VOWS,** by
Margaret Moore (Harlequin Historical #248),
coming in December.

HOLLYWOOD

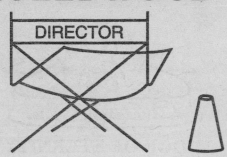

Coming this Fall—
Harlequin Movies on TV!

If you like a good romance you'll *love* the brand-new Harlequin movies that will be airing on the CBS network on Sunday afternoons this Fall!

These full-length *romantic* movies are based on Harlequin novels written by some of your favorite authors! They're entertaining romances with lots of twists and turns and guaranteed to keep you riveted to your seat, so watch for them!

As a Reader Service member you'll be hearing more about these Harlequin movies in the months to come. Next month's *Heart to Heart* newsletter, for example, will bring you more specific details, along with information about the exciting prizes you could win in the all new

"Harlequin Goes to Hollywood" Sweepstakes!

CBSBPA

Fifty red-blooded, white-hot, true-blue hunks
from every State in the Union!

Look for MEN MADE IN AMERICA! Written by some
of our most popular authors, these stories feature fifty
of the strongest, sexiest men, each from a different state
in the union!

Two titles available every month at your favorite
retail outlet.

In October, look for:

CHOICES by Annette Broadrick (Missouri)
PART OF THE BARGAIN by Linda Lael Miller
(Montana)

In November, look for:

SECRETS OF TYRONE by Regan Forest (Nebraska)
NOBODY'S BABY by Barbara Bretton (Nevada)

You won't be able to resist MEN MADE IN AMERICA!